American

Honey

Also by Nancy Scrofano

True Love Way

Cupid On Deck

Happenstance

Ice Dating

American Honey

NANCY SCROFANO

Moonwood Books

AMERICAN HONEY
ISBN-13: 978-0-6159315-0-0
Bloomwood Books
For inquiries, please visit www.bloomwoodbooks.com.

For my mom. Always.

American Honey

One

I'm the secret that nobody knows.

"What's your name?" I drawl, gawking at the boy next to me in the line. Waiting for him to respond, I tilt my head back to study the waves in his reddish brown hair, then eye his crimson plaid shirt, rugged taper jeans, and boots black as coal.

He glances over at me, removing his music player's ear bud from his left side in one swift motion. "Jack. What's yours?"

"Olivia. Where're you from?" I peer into his narrow eyes of sparkly, light blue.

"Chapel Hill, up in Carolina. You?"

"Summerville, here in Georgia. About two hours away. He nods, even though it isn't clear if he's ever heard of my small town. Then, he focuses again on the music player hooked onto his pants pocket.

"How old are you?" I continue on.

Jack cracks a little smile, giving me a sideways glance. "How old do I look?"

I examine his face carefully. "Sixteen."

"Nope."

"Well, then, how old?"

"Just turned nineteen yesterday."

My eyes light up. "I can sing happy birthday to you, if you like." I bat my eyelashes to entice him to say yes.

He glances around, his cheeks reddening from my proposed serenade. "Thanks, but that won't be necessary."

"Okay." I let him off the hook. "But I'll have you know that I do the best rendition of the birthday song in all of Chattooga County."

Jack smiles. "I'll take your word for it."

"You know what?" I press on. "You have a baby face."

"Uh, thanks?" he replies, shrugging.

I place my hand on his shoulder. "Don't worry. It'll be a good thing when you're older."

He laughs, shaking his head. "You sure like to talk a lot. How old are you?"

"Eighteen, but my granddaddy says I sound much older when I sing," I explain to Jack, grinning with pride.

"People say the same to me." He angles his head with a crooked smile. He's awkward, but I'm drawn to him and his deep, southern drawl. Jack's voice doesn't match his boyish exterior, which ramps up my desire to hear his singing chops.

"What kind of music do you sing?"

"Country."

"Me, too!" I exclaim with my usual bubbly enthusiasm, appreciating that he's a boy after my own heart. "I can't wait to sing in the Fox Theatre. I'm tired of waiting in this darn line."

"There's a lot of hanging around. I'll tell you what. I'm just glad I made it through the preliminaries yesterday." Jack relaxes his shoulders, letting out a long breath.

"I know. I was so nervous! I don't usually get jittery before I sing, but I've never been in a contest like this before."

"Me neither."

"How long have you been singing?"

Jack studies the ceiling, obviously giving my question some thought. "Uh, since I was about five. You?"

"Oh, a long, long time. Probably since I could talk. My mama bought me a karaoke machine when I was real little, and I would sing whenever anyone came to our house." I pause, thinking back. "You know, I would sing for just about anyone. Anyone at all. No matter where we were. I still do that. I'm always singing, or talking, or singing, or talking." I can't help but laugh.

"Apparently," Jack says, nodding with a small chuckle.

"Are you here alone?" I ask, changing the subject. I have a habit of saying whatever pops into my head. I'm not afraid of asking anyone anything.

"Nope. I came with two of my boys from back home; my cousin, Ryder, and my friend, Brett."

"Where are they?"

Jack's eyes dart back and forth over my head. "Oh, they're around here somewhere. Just waiting for me to go on."

"Are you in college?" I can't put my finger on the reason why, but I want to know everything about Jack. I feel connected to him already.

His eyes go wide. "Am I on trial?"

I step back, pouting. "I'm just making conversation." I turn away, wondering if my initial attraction to him was a mistake. Maybe he doesn't want to shoot the breeze with me.

"Hey," he says in that smooth, low voice, grabbing my attention again. "I just graduated high school."

I jerk my head around to see kindness reappear in his bright eyes. He *does* want to chat with me. Maybe he's just shy. I guess I can be sort of overwhelming for a bashful person. One of the seamstresses who works at my mama's store seemed really frightened by me when she first met me a few years ago. She hardly ever made eye contact with me and avoided conversations when I went into the store after school. I won her over, though. I always win people over. *Always.*

"Me, too. This is sort of like a graduation trip for me and my best friend, Hanna. My older sister, Kat, is here, too. Well, she's only two years older than me. We're pretty close." I notice that Jack is grinning at me again. I'm rambling on and on, like usual.

He doesn't stop me, though. He seems interested, as near as I can tell.

The contest wranglers start calling contestants into the theater. They make their way down the line, getting awfully close to me and Jack. A surge of nerves bolts through my stomach since I'll soon be singing on stage in the historic Fox Theatre. All I can think about is belting my heart out and claiming the victory. The winner gets ten thousand dollars, and the runner up gets five thousand dollars. But second place isn't really on my radar. I'm in Atlanta to win.

As we get closer to going inside the theater, I notice that the participants have to stop at a booth and talk to a camera before they're escorted inside. I can't hear exactly what they're saying to the camera because of the other contestants' noisy chatter. The jitters return, my whole body tensing up like one giant clenched fist.

"You don't like being on camera?" Jack catches me staring at the booth with just-saw-a-ghost eyes.

"I like live audiences. I'm not used to talking to a camera lens. My mama always films my performances, but that's different." I size up the other contestants, my eyes sweeping the room from person to person.

Some of them are here with their parents. Maybe I should have asked my mama to come with me. But Hanna told me that since we graduated high school, we couldn't rely on our parents all the time anymore. At least she has two parents to depend on. It's just my mama, Kat, and me, and it's been that way for a long time. My daddy left us when we were real little. He's a drummer, or at least he *was* a drummer. I have no idea what he's doing now. My mama always tells us that musicians never stick around. She says, "A different city every night is no way to raise a family."

I often wonder if I'll be like my daddy. I can't help it, though. Music will always be my life. I don't know what the future holds for me, but standing in this line, I'm certain of one thing no matter what Hanna said. I miss my mama.

Jack gives me an encouraging nod. "You'll be fine. Ain't nothing to it. You just gotta do it."

I really like his advice. He's so calm and cool about everything. I'm not as terrified when I look into his eyes. "Thanks," I whisper.

A young guy, with hair a few shades darker than Jack's, approaches us. He's wearing an Atlanta Idol T-shirt, faded jeans, and sneakers caked with dried mud. I notice the bags under his eyes and that his nametag says "Jimmy."

"You're up next, man," Jimmy tells Jack in a monotone voice. "Step in front of the camera and say your full name, age, where you're from, and why you're the next Atlanta Idol."

Jack does as he's told and stands there at ease with loose posture while he waits to get his cue to start talking.

"I'm Jack Bradley. I'm nineteen years old, and I'm from Chapel Hill, North Carolina," Jack reveals to the camera after Jimmy gives him the okay. "I'm the next Atlanta Idol because I believe I have a God-given talent that I'm meant to share with people. If I win, I plan to put the money toward my professional singing career. I want to use my voice to change people's lives, and Atlanta Idol is the first step toward achieving that goal."

I stare in awe at Jack. He radiates maturity and self-assurance. His answer isn't rehearsed or forced. He's a natural in front of the camera. When he moves out of the way, Jimmy approaches me next.

"Your turn," he informs me.

I take a deep breath, inching toward the camera. I have no idea what to say. Why do I want to be the next Atlanta Idol? The obvious answer is that I love to sing, but I can't just say that, can I? I'm sure they want more. My palms are slick, and my knees are wobbling like a baby bird's legs after it leaves the nest for the first time. My mind races, desperately trying to figure out what to say until the moment is upon me.

"My name is Olivia McKenna, but everyone calls me Ollie. I'm eighteen years old, and I'm from Summerville, Georgia. I want to be the next Atlanta Idol because I love to sing." I pause for a second. Behind the cameraman, I see Kat and Hanna smiling and waving at me. With their support, I grin in return and continue. "I've been singing since I could talk. I love Georgia. Born and raised here. All I've ever wanted to do is sing for people. That's why I would be a great Atlanta Idol." I breathe a huge sigh of relief when Jimmy gives me the thumbs up sign.

"Nice job," Jack compliments me as we head into the theater. He had been waiting off to the side to see how I did. What a kindhearted boy.

"How's it going, sweetie?" Kat stops me, her emerald eyes flashing with concern, and Jack goes on ahead. Her oversized sunglasses are perched atop her super short, bleached blonde hair. "We went to get something to eat. Are you hungry or are you about to go on?" She's holding a Dairy Queen cup in one hand and the car keys in the other.

"I think I'm singing soon." I glance around, my whole body overcome with nerves. "I better go."

"Okay, we'll grab seats and wait for your performance," Hanna chimes in. "How many of y'all are singing in this round?"

"I'm not sure exactly. I guess we'll see." I muster up the best smile I can, trying to control my anxiety.

Kat wraps me up in a hug. "You'll be great, Oll. Good luck!"

"Isn't it break a leg?" Hanna asks Kat.

"I don't know! Means the same thing. Come on!" Kat grabs Hanna's arm and leads her down the aisle as Hanna turns slightly, flipping her long, chocolate brown hair, to blow me a kiss.

"I love y'all!" I call after them. I get that warm, fuzzy feeling inside knowing they're in the audience, but the nerves still gnaw at me.

Despite the noise-filled room buzzing with contestants, I'm suddenly aware of the raw emotions bubbling up inside me. The other people are all kinds. Some are polished with real fancy clothes while others look like they just came from working on a farm. Most of them have a youthful energy, but they probably aren't my age. It's hard to tell. Do any of them long for a hug from their mama the way I do? I'm alone in a crowd, and soon I'll be by my lonesome onstage in *front* of a crowd. But then they'll all know my name and my voice. And that's what I've always wanted, right?

"Lord, help me," I whisper.

Two

In the contestant section of the theater, I settle in next to Jack. We both have our numbers that the staff gave us pinned to the front of our shirts. Jack told me that they'll call us one by one onto the stage to sing our songs. This is the individual round of performances. Yesterday, I submitted the song I'm going to sing so that the music will be cued up for my performance.

"What are you singing?" Jack queries me, his eyes twinkling with curiosity.

"'Jesus Take the Wheel' by Carrie Underwood. I love the message of the song." I stop for a second to think of the lyrics, silently praying that I won't forget them when I'm onstage. "Are you religious?"

Jack holds out the small cross on a chain around his neck and smiles. "Yes, ma'am."

"Good, because I'm going to need all the prayers I can get while I'm up there."

"You'll be fine. You said you love to sing for anyone and everyone. So, sing. Just sing like you would anywhere else." Jack relaxes into his seat and folds his hands across his stomach.

"How come you aren't nervous?"

"I bet I will be right before I sing, but for now, I'm just trying to enjoy the experience. It'll all be over in two shakes of a sheep's tail."

I sit back in my seat and try to mirror Jack's confidence, despite my mind racing with lyrics and melodies.

We watch a lot of other contestants perform their songs before us. Some are really good, so good that the audience erupts into applause, including a few standing ovations. It takes everything in me not to race right out of the theater. I worry that they're better than me. Maybe I'm not cut out for this. But then there are other performances that are just mediocre, which boosts my confidence slightly. My anxiety aside, I'm determined to win. I have to remember that. *I want to win.* I begin repeating it silently to myself so I can focus.

Atlanta Idol is technically a local competition, but because of the Internet, it's well known. Every summer for the past eight years, people come from around the country to try out. Music producers and managers are always in the audience for the final rounds, and I don't think this time will be any different. I *have* to make the finals.

Jack takes the stage, telling the panel of judges, four members of the Atlanta performing arts community, that he'll be singing "Kiss A Girl" by Keith Urban. The music bursts through the speakers, and Jack croons that kissing and telling isn't his style. I can't help but giggle. He sings the first verse with a quiet confidence, then gets more into it at the chorus.

People in the audience are all smiles, clapping along. Jack *owns* that stage. He moves from one side to the other, declaring that he wants to kiss a girl. This boy has such teen heartthrob appeal from the way he moves his body to the music, to the way he just barely touches the microphone to his lips while he makes eye contact with every girl in the front row and beyond. Jack is working the room. His voice is strong with a range that any singer would envy. It's so unexpected given his boy-next-door looks and reserved demeanor.

Before I know it, the song reaches its conclusion, and I'm the only one in the audience not standing. I jump from my seat and join in the thunderous applause that echo throughout the theater.

"That was amazing! Boy, you sure can sing!" I squeal as Jack approaches our seats.

"It sounded okay?" He doesn't seem even the slightest bit phased by the crowd's reaction. He appears unsure. He looks like me. *Nervous*.

"Are you kidding? It was better than okay. It was incredible!" I study his face, and he finally meets my eyes and shrugs. "Are you anxious *after* performing? I don't get it."

Jack raises his shoulders with uncertainty again as he puts his earphones in. "It's over, but it's not really over, ya know? I want to make the next round."

"What are you doing now?"

"Listening to the songs I'm fixing to sing. Gotta keep running them through my head. Don't want to be caught with my pants down." He pushes play, turns up the volume, and shuts his eyes while the other contestants take the stage.

My turn is coming up. I search for Kat and Hanna but don't spot them. Making my way to the wings to wait, I hum "Jesus Take the Wheel." My body trembles. My throat is parched like I haven't had water in days, but I guzzled down an entire bottle only an hour ago. I'm itching to flee again, but as I eye the stage before me, I know there's no turning back now. I'm going to do this. I have to do this, even if my mama isn't in favor of it. I have to do this so that people can hear me, *really* hear me. It's my turn to standout. But most of all, I have to do this to prove to myself that I can. I'm tired of being stuck at the back of the line.

The judges call my number, and I exchange anxious smiles with the girl standing next to me who's also waiting her turn. While we were passing the time, I told her how pretty her wavy auburn hair looks with her pale yellow sundress. Like a proper Southern belle, she returned the compliment, saying she loves my floral print maxi dress and my thick, blonde highlights that weave through my chestnut curls. She sure is a sweetheart, and chatting with her helped lessen the thick layer of anxious tension looming over us.

The crowd welcomes me with applause as I inch my way to the middle of the stage in my peep toe, suede wedges. The spotlight is intense, almost blinding. I can barely see the judges or anyone else. My song starts playing at full volume, and I hang onto the microphone for dear life with both of my clammy hands. Swiftly launching into the first verse, I share a story that Carrie Underwood always tells so well. My voice is timid and the notes are careful, the music threatening to overpower me. I've never felt more vulnerable than I do in this moment as I stare into the vast darkness beyond the glaring lights. But just like the woman in the song, I eventually decide to let Jesus take the wheel. When I get to the chorus, I release one of my hands from the microphone and slowly raise it in the air, closing my eyes. The nerves gradually leave my body as the music, the message, and the emotion claim my performance and envelope the room.

After hitting the last note and softly bringing the song to a close, I'm shocked by what's happening. My eyes brim with tears, and an overwhelming sensation of gratitude fills my still tingling body. The audience is standing. And applauding. Loudly. *For me.*

Back at the hotel that night, Hanna, Kat, and I go to the rooftop pool to hang out with the other contestants. Jack is there with his cousin, Ryder, and his friend, Brett. I'm tuckered out from the day, but too wired from my performance to sleep. Hanna and Kat chat with some of the contestants, mostly with the boys since they're both such flirts. I'm usually right there with them flirting and talk, talk, talking, but tonight I want a minute to myself to take it all in. Am I really part of Atlanta Idol? Am I really here? I need to pinch myself. My performance had gone unbelievably well.

I want to call my mama to tell her all about it, but she's probably already asleep. After I finished singing, only a few more singers were left, and then we were all called back onto the stage in groups of ten. The judges told us who out of each group would be staying and who would be going home. Jack and I both made it to the next round, but we were in different groups. I haven't seen much of him until now. Hanna and Kat took me to dinner for bacon cheeseburgers and sweet tea to celebrate.

I'm at the far end of the pool, sugary iced drink still in hand, admiring the city.

"Great view," Jack says, appearing next to me.

I glance up at him and into those luminous blue eyes that seem so familiar, even though we only met a few hours before. "Yeah. Atlanta's beautiful."

His mouth opens like he's about to say something, but he closes it, turning to look at the skyline instead.

We're quiet for a few minutes, enjoying the refreshing breeze that's unusual for summer in Georgia.

I start humming "This Little Light of Mine," marveling at the dazzling city lights and the stars peeking through the thick black sky. When I turn to Jack, he's watching me, his lips curled up into a lighthearted smile.

"My daddy and I used to sing that song together. We would sit out on the porch and try to find the constellations in the night sky. I loved when he sang to me."

"You don't sing with him anymore?" Jack asks, his brow creasing with curiosity. The flicker of sadness in his eyes reveals that he's already guessed the answer.

I shake my head. "He left us a long time ago. He's a touring musician. A drummer. I have no idea which band he plays in now. I never hear from him." A wave of relief washes over me after sharing that with Jack. Even though it's an unpleasant fact that still bothers me to this day, I want to be honest with him from the get-go about my background, and I hope he'll do the same.

Jack moves closer to me like he wants to comfort me but doesn't know how. "It's his loss," he says simply.

I release a disappointed sigh. "Mine, too."

He gazes into my eyes, and I feel the same spark as earlier when we were standing in line at the contest. "You were amazing today." As soon as the compliment leaves his mouth, he jerks his head toward the city again, focusing on something in the distance.

I smile shyly. "Think so?"

"Definitely."

I study the side of his face, wishing I could trace my fingers along the hint of stubble covering his jawline. I don't want to look away in hopes that he'll meet my eyes again, but Hanna, Kat, Ryder, and Brett interrupt us.

"Are we going in the water or what?" Ryder asks. He has short, toffee brown hair, eyes that match, and similar features to Jack's. There's a family resemblance for sure. He's cute, but Jack is cuter.

"I guess so," Jack replies. "Oh. Uh, Ollie, this is Ryder, and that's Brett."

"Nice to meet you both," I say as we grin at each other.

Brett is a smidge taller than Jack and Ryder. I notice how his golden hair flops down onto his forehead when he raises his eyebrows to acknowledge me. He has a five o'clock shadow obscuring his square chin. He's attractive, too, but Jack is more attractive. In my opinion, at least.

"I think we'll just hang out over here and relax," Kat declares, pointing to the lounge chairs lining the pool area.

Hanna and I agree, sitting down to watch as Jack, Ryder, and Brett remove their shirts and cannonball into the pool. They're all athletically built, which reminds me that I should ask Jack which sports he likes to play. I want to ask him lots of things. There's so much more I want to know about Jack. I really hope I'll get the chance.

Three

The next morning, I arrive at the Fox a little before eight o'clock. Hanna and Kat are having breakfast while I attend rehearsal for the duo/group round of the competition. The contest staff explains to all the remaining contestants that we have to form either a duo or a group, and we'll have until one o'clock to practice with each other. Then, we have to return to the theater at four o'clock to perform. That doesn't give us very much time at all. This contest is much more stressful than I ever imagined. I hope I didn't bite off more than I can chew.

Once the crew finishes giving us instructions, they let us find a partner or a group to join. Immediately, I think of Jack and how much I want to sing with him. Hopefully, he hasn't already found a partner or joined a group before I get the chance to ask him. I start looking around the group of about fifty people, finally spotting Jack three rows behind me talking to another contestant. I scurry over to him.

"Hey, y'all! Good morning!" I say in a hurry, smiling politely at Jack and the guy next to him. "Jack, can I talk to you?"

He excuses himself from his conversation and walks up the aisle with me. "Yeah, I was just going to look for you."

"Really?" I squeak.

"Mmhmm. Want to pair up for this round?"

I nod repeatedly. "That's what I was going to ask you." I rest my hand on his arm. "We're like two peas in a pod."

"I guess so," Jack agrees, grinning at me. "We need to decide real soon what to sing."

On our way out of the theater, Jack picks up a book of songs that we can choose from since the music is readily available for them. We go into the lobby and find an area away from the other contestants to sit down and figure out our song.

"Let's look at the country section," I suggest, turning the pages. "You want to sing a country song, right?"

"Mmhmm." Jack sits next to me, peering over my shoulder at the list. He's close enough for me to drink in the scent of his cologne. It reminds me of the ocean air at Myrtle Beach, down in Carolina, where my mama used to take me and Kat every summer.

"How about 'Louisiana Woman, Mississippi Man' by Conway Twitty and Loretta Lynn?" I ask, pointing to it on the list as I glance up at Jack. "It's a classic, and it's fun."

He refuses with his head. "I don't think so. We should go for something more modern and maybe not as corny." He pauses for a second. "Wait a minute. You know Conway Twitty and Loretta Lynn?"

At first, I gape at him in response to his crazy question. "Of course! I grew up listening to them. My mama loves their duets. I do, too."

"Y'all have that in common with my mom."

"I think every country music fan has that in common." I skim the page for more songs, turning it when I don't see anything quite right. "How about a Faith Hill and Tim McGraw duet? Maybe 'I Need You'?"

Jack blushes, averting his eyes from mine. "Nah. Too much."

"Come on. You could sell it. It's just for the stage." I touch his shoulder to get his attention. "Don't be shy."

"I'm not. It's just... Let's move on." He means business with a stern expression across his face.

"I didn't mean to ruffle your feathers. We'll pick something else."

His face relaxes, and he laughs for a second, glancing back down at the list. "Lady Antebellum? They're current and popular."

"Yes, sir. I love them! Which song?" I let out a giggle. "I think 'Need You Now' is out of the question."

"You making fun of me?" Jack asks, chuckling again, too. "These country artists sure are needy."

We both burst out laughing. Jack is incredibly focused, but he has a funny side to him, too. He makes me laugh when I least expect him to, which I like about him. I think our personalities balance each other out in a really good way. I'm more in your face, chatting and making jokes, and he's subtler about how he communicates with people.

"That's it!" I exclaim, pointing to Lady Antebellum's "American Honey."

"Mm. Yeah, I like that song. I can dig it," Jack agrees.

It's settled. Our duet will be "American Honey," and we're both over the moon about it. Jack and I retrieve our music from the staff and venture into the Egyptian Ballroom to start rehearsing. The space is separated into sections by partitions so that each duo and group can have some privacy, but it's still noisy with everyone trying to work out their songs in the same area. From the turquoise carpet with ancient detailed patterns, to the massive columns and elaborate fireplace, the room resembles something I'd find in one of the history books at school. The yellowy lights are on, but there's a darkness that's almost eerie. After a few minutes, Jack and I go outside to the terrace to rehearse instead. We use my notebook computer, a graduation gift from my granddaddy, to get the lyrics.

"I think I should sing the first verse. That changes it up a bit," Jack suggests to me. He starts singing to show me how it would go.

I bob my head along in agreement. "That sounded good. I'll take the second verse." I scroll down to my part, belting out the lyrics as I read them.

"Yeah. I like that," Jack says. "Let's sing the chorus and the bridge together."

We practice the verses a few times but work the most on the parts we have to sing together. It's easier than I expected to harmonize with Jack. I've never sung a duet with anyone before, but our voices blend together naturally. Maybe it's a sign that this competition will work out well for me. We rehearse for hours until just before one o'clock when we take a break. Other duos and groups start leaving the theater for the three-hour hiatus until performance time.

Jack and I sit on the ground of the terrace with our backs leaning on the wall. I log into my Twitter account to update my friends and family on the contest while Jack text messages Ryder.

"You use Twitter?" Jack asks, taking a peek at my screen.

"Yeah. Do you?"

"@JaxBradley"

"Jax?"

"It's a nickname my baseball team gave to me. I've been playing ever since I could hit and throw a ball," Jack reveals. "I forget exactly who started it, but the nickname stuck."

I smile at him. "I like it."

"What's your Twitter name?"

"@OllieMcKenna"

"Does everyone call you Ollie, not Olivia?"

"Yeah, mostly." I laugh before adding, "My mama only calls me Olivia when I've been up to no good."

"Does that happen often?" he wonders, a tiny grin curving his lips.

I shake my head. "No, sir. I'm a lady."

Our eyes meet with equal glimmers of curiosity and playfulness.

"Got it," Jack replies, breaking our stare and focusing on his phone again. "Ryder and Brett are coming to pick me up. We're going to Bojangles for lunch. You want to come?"

"That sounds great! I go to Bojangles all the time when I'm in Rome. That's where my mama's store is located. I go there a lot after school. Well, I used to since school's over now. She owns a clothing boutique. It's really adorable and—" I realize that I'm talking Jack's ear off again and all he did was ask me to lunch.

He doesn't seem to mind though, studying me with inquisitive eyes and that grin that I enjoy more and more every time I see it.

"Uh, let me see what Kat and Hanna are up to first." I quickly fire a text message to Kat asking for their whereabouts.

"Okay," Jack says as he rises to his feet.

Within seconds, Kat replies, and I relay her message to Jack. "She said that she's in Olympic Park with Hanna listening to live music. They already saw the fountain show." I frown after reading her message. It sounds like they're having a great time sightseeing, and I'm stuck rehearsing all day. But I know I have to make sacrifices if I'm ever going to have a music career, so I'm not about to complain.

Besides, if I have to rehearse, I'm glad I'm with Jack. It doesn't feel like a chore. When he's around, it's more fun than a basket full of puppies.

I grab my bag and stand up. "They'll either meet us at Bojangles or meet up with us later. Can I ride with you guys?"

"Sure." Jack opens the door for me to go into the Grand Salon, another historic ballroom with impressive detail from floor to ceiling, so we can exit the theater. He's such a gentleman, but I don't expect anything less. Manners are a staple around these parts.

It's quite the adventure getting from the Fox to Bojangles. Brett's driving Jack's truck and refuses to admit that he doesn't know exactly where he's going. It should only take us about a half hour if there isn't too much traffic, but it's shaping up to take much longer, even without bad traffic. I swear it's like Brett is driving in circles. It seems like we're passing the same signs over and over again.

Jack is up front with Brett, and Ryder and I are in the backseat. Jack is fit to be tied with Brett and lamenting the faulty navigation system, and I have to turn toward my window when I want to laugh. There's just something funny about Brett and Jack having a serious argument about the location of a Bojangles. I don't know Ryder well enough yet to share a laugh with him, and he isn't talking much to me anyway. He's a backseat driver involved in the "Where's Bojangles?" debate. Then, Brett seriously asks Jack, "What's your Bodar telling you?" That does it. My laughter is uncontrollable now.

Jack turns around, frustration written all over his face, but his expression softens when he sees me guffawing. "Can one of y'all get the directions from your phone? My battery is running low."

I should have thought of that sooner, but I've been too wrapped up in the hilarious dynamic between these three boys. "Okay," I say. "Y'all need to get the GPS fixed. How on earth did you get all the way here from Chapel Hill? You can't even make it across town!"

"I was driving," Jack responds with pride. "Usually, I have an incredible sense of direction."

"Actually, I drove, too," Ryder adds, turning to me. "And we have a map. It just doesn't have fast food places on it."

"Y'all think they sell Bojangles maps?" Brett asks.

Everyone laughs at the question. Brett is funny when he doesn't mean to be. Or maybe he is the class clown type. I'm not exactly sure, but I do know that I want to hang out with these boys more often, especially Jack.

Maybe I'm jumping the gun, but I've already set my cap for him.

Four

When we finally make it to Bojangles, we settle into a booth with our fried chicken, biscuits, and sweet tea.

"It's finally Bo time, y'all," Brett exclaims as we start to devour our food.

Jack savors each bite of his chicken. "Mmhmm."

"How long have y'all been friends?" I ask before taking a sip of my sugary thirst-quencher.

Ryder sets his gravy biscuit down. "Jack and I met Brett in preschool. All in the same class and all about the same age. I'm eighteen and Brett's nineteen like Jack."

"I'm turning nineteen next week," I inform them. "When's your birthday, Ryder?"

"Next week, too. Wednesday."

"Mine's on Friday. Imagine that! We should have a party." I beam at them and grab a fry.

Jack chuckles. "That'd be fun. Too bad you'll be back in Summerville, and we'll be up in Carolina by then."

Disappointment gnaws at me, twisting my stomach into a knot. I know we'll go our separate ways at the end of the week when Atlanta Idol is over, but since I'm having a good time with them, I almost forgot that we don't live near each other.

"Well, we better keep in touch. Don't forget about your duet partner," I say to Jack.

He gives me a timid smile. "I won't forget you. I don't think I could, even if I tried."

Heat bolts to my cheeks. Does that mean he likes me? Maybe he's just being kind.

"Promise?" I ask.

"Promise."

"Pinky swear?"

"Ollie. Come on." Jack rolls his eyes and laughs.

I like the way he says my name with his thick North Carolina accent. Still determined, I hold my pinky finger out across the table. "Well?"

Jack reluctantly locks his finger with mine. An unfamiliar rush rockets through my whole body when our fingers touch. His face turns bright red, and I suspect mine has gone and done the same. I let go in a hurry, my eyes darting to my food as bashfulness creeps over me. Maybe Jack is rubbing off on me. Or maybe I like him. Like *really* like him. Immediately, I tell myself that's ridiculous, especially since it isn't likely we'll ever see each other again after this week.

My cell phone buzzes in my bag, so I yank it out, revealing a text message from Hanna saying they're on their way to Bojangles. Another rush swooshes from my head to my toes when I take note of the time. *Panic.*

"Kat and Hanna are on their way, but we have to get back to the theater soon or we'll be late. I want to rehearse our song some more, too," I tell Jack.

"It's okay. Let's finish up, and then we'll head back. It's all good." His calm, cool attitude is back again.

I pretend to play it cool, but I'm freaking out inside. I don't want to be late. We don't know yet when we'll be called onstage. What if they call our number and we aren't there? That would be a complete disaster, ruining any chance we have of advancing. I push my plate away. I'm not hungry anymore. I have to get back to that theater. The boys must sense my anxiety because they finish eating right quick. Then again, teenage boys are known for wolfing down their food. Either way, I'm thankful.

"Should we wait here for Kat and Hanna?" Ryder wonders when we all make our way out to the parking lot.

I text Hanna again to see where they are, and she says they're really close. I relay the message to the boys. "Jack, we better rehearse here while we wait."

"Here? In the parking lot?"

"Sure. Why not?"

A few minutes later, the truck's doors are wide open, and our music is turned up on the stereo. Jack and I are sitting in the bed of his royal blue Ford F-150 practicing "American Honey." When it's my turn to sing, Jack nods his head along to the music and drums his fingertips to the beat. My eyes wander up from his fingers to his toned arms that glisten in the sun. Distracted by studying every inch of him, I almost forget the words. During the chorus we lock eyes, and I'm afraid I might just melt into a puddle of goo right there. It's always been my dream to sing, but now this cute boy makes it even better. People gather around the truck, random passersby stopping and customers inside the restaurant coming outside to hear us sing. I share a look of disbelief with Jack, but he gestures for me to keep singing. When we finish the song, the small crowd cheers.

"Sing another song!" someone shouts.

"Yeah, y'all are real good!" another voice yells out.

Glancing around at all the faces in front of me, it begins to sink in that people are actually waiting for us to sing some more. They're smiling and talking amongst themselves. I realize that this is what it would be like to have an audience for my own show. No judges. No contest on the line. No winning or losing. Just people who want to hear me sing. I want this so bad. Then, it dawns on me that I have it right here in front of me in the Bojangles parking lot. No matter where I am, I'm a singer. I, Ollie McKenna, am a *singer*.

"This is the only song we've practiced together. We're in the Atlanta Idol competition," I share with everyone. "It's for the duo/group round. We can sing it again." I grin enthusiastically at all the new faces as they clap and signal their approval. "Ready?" I ask Jack.

"Mmhmm."

Brett climbs in the truck and starts the music again from the top. During our encore of "American Honey," I notice Kat's silver Jeep Grand Cherokee pulling into the parking lot. She and Hanna jump out and join the group near Jack's truck.

When the music ends, everyone hoots and hollers for us again. "Thank y'all!" I shout.

"Yeah, thank y'all so much!" Jack echoes.

I turn to Jack. "We better get going."

He agrees and helps me out of the back of his truck. I do my best to ignore that tingly sensation I get when he grabs my hand. Some people are still hanging around and wish me and Jack good luck at Atlanta Idol.

"Y'all were great!" Hanna chirps, approaching us. She gives me a big hug, then I step aside while she pats Jack on the back. "I'm so glad we got to hear you rehearse. We might not be at the performance later."

I jerk my head in her direction. "What do you mean? Why not?"

"When we were at Olympic Park, there was a contest to win four Braves tickets for tonight's game, and we won!" Kat explains, standing next to Hanna now. "By the way, y'all were terrific. Maybe us winning tickets is a sign that y'all will win Atlanta Idol." She looks back and forth between me and Jack with wide, enthusiastic eyes.

Jack and I exchange an awkward glance before he suddenly finds the pavement incredibly interesting.

"Only one person will win," he mutters with downcast eyes.

I know there will only be one winner, but when Jack says it out loud, reality sets in. Maybe I'll win, or maybe Jack will win, or maybe neither of us will even come close. I have no idea what will happen, but I'm anxious just thinking about it.

"That's true. But it has to be a good sign, right?" Kat smiles at us.

I avoid everyone's awkward glances. "I guess. I hope so." I pause for a second. "What are you gonna do with the other two tickets? You said you won four."

"We thought Brett and Ryder could come along," Hanna says, looking over my shoulder to where Brett and Ryder are standing.

Ryder steps forward next to Jack. "Count us in."

Hanna and Kat grin, clearly satisfied.

"The game's at seven, so we might miss you guys singing, depending when you get called," Kat adds.

"Okay, Ollie and I better get going," Jack announces, glancing at his cell phone and then at me. "We can go back to the theater together." He flicks his eyes to Brett and Ryder. "Can y'all catch a ride with Hanna and Kat?"

"Sure," Brett agrees.

It's all settled. Jack and I are on our own to head back to the contest. I really want Hanna and Kat to be there, but I know this is their vacation, too, and they deserve to have some fun. I can't imagine that sitting in a theater listening to amateur singers all night is their idea of a great time, but I also thought they came to support me. We say our goodbyes, and I take a deep breath as I watch everyone except me and Jack pile into Kat's Jeep.

"Ollie?" Jack is holding the passenger door open, waiting for me to get in.

I give him a small smile as I climb inside. Soon after, he jumps behind the wheel and turns the stereo up on our way out of the parking lot. Jason Aldean's "Dirt Road Anthem" blares as we head for the highway.

"Looks like it's just you and me, kid," Jack says, flashing me a quick grin. He has one hand resting on the top of the steering wheel and the other hanging out the window. He sings along to the song, knowing all the words. Color me impressed.

Trying not to gawk at him, I sneak a quick smile. In this moment, I'm pretty sure I'm crushing on Jack. That makes me even more nervous for our duet. I just hope I can pull it off and look cool as a cucumber, like he always does.

♫

Around six thirty, Jack and I wait in the wings at the theater, anticipating our performance. I got a text from Hanna that they all came by the theater and stayed for an hour, but left to go to the baseball game just after six o'clock. Jack and I didn't see them, but that's probably because we were in the contestant holding area until now. I'm sad that they're going to miss our duet, but I have to put it out of my mind so I can concentrate on our song. Jack suggests that we pray together before going onstage. We share a moment to ourselves, holding hands and asking the Lord for a good performance. As we watch the group before us get comments from the judges, the butterflies in my stomach grow by leaps and bounds, taking over like the tail wagging the dog.

I literally lean on Jack for support, resting my head on his shoulder. "I'm scared, Jack," I whisper.

He gently puts his arm around my waist. "It's okay. Ain't nothin' to be frightened of out there. Just sing to me."

We lock eyes, and for that brief moment, I feel a sense of safety. Then, the judges call our number, so Jack leads the way onto the stage. When we get out there, my knees are about to buckle, and my heart's pounding in my ears and pulsating all over like I'm about to explode. As the music for "American Honey" booms through the auditorium, Jack holds my gaze and nods just like he did when we sang at Bojangles. Whenever our eyes meet, the tension in my body eases up, despite my possible crush on him. Jack and I have some sort of connection that I can't quite put my finger on. It's like I've known this boy my whole life, and it only makes sense to do what he says. He told me to sing to him, so I am. We're completely in sync. I forget about the crowd, crooning like there's no one else in the room but Jack. Nothing matters besides the music and our voices. We're in our own little world, just the two of us. When we finish the song, it happens again. I'm overcome with emotion, my vision cloudy from tears. Through blurry eyes, I squint at the audience and notice every single person standing. The roar of everyone cheering is so loud that I'm certain I'll never forget this sound as long as I live. Jack and I exchange surprised glances, our faces lit up by the bright stage lights but more so by the thrill of it all. We stare in awe at the crowd of people as we wait for feedback from the judges.

Jack leans over to me and speaks slowly into my ear with his sweet Southern drawl. "You did it, baby."

Five

"You were completely connected to the music, the lyrics, and most importantly to each other. I adore both of you," one of the judges gushes to me and Jack.

Another judge leans forward in his seat, staring intently at us. "I agree. There's something special going on here. You two have that 'it' factor."

The other two judges echo these comments and tell us that Jack and I are "going places." We thank them several times, then excitedly hurry off the stage.

"Can you believe it?" I ask Jack on our way back to the contestant holding area.

Jack laughs, shaking his head. "This is wild."

"Think we'll make the next round?"

"I have a good feeling, but we shouldn't count our chickens until they hatch."

I nod, agreeing with Jack, but I can't help feeling more confident. I'm so happy that even if we don't make the next round, that duet is a heck of a way to go out.

Later that night, we're back on stage with the other contestants as the judges narrow down the group to the top fifteen. Jack and I stand next to each other, waiting to hear the news. With only three spots left in the top fifteen, one of the judges says, "Ollie McKenna, please step forward. You made it to the next round." I jump up and then hug Jack so hard we almost fall over.

I move to the front of the stage, but worry replaces my excitement when I glance back at Jack, who is still waiting to hear if he gets one of the last two spots. Our eyes connect, and he shrugs with just a flicker of a smile.

Going forward in the competition without Jack is unimaginable. I want to go to the next round so badly, and I am, but I want to be there with Jack. The judges call the name of the next contestant to make it, and it isn't Jack's. I hold my breath, praying that Jack's name is last. I can't look at him. Not focusing on anything in particular, I stare out at the empty seats, biting my lip while waiting for the judges to speak. Seconds feel like hours until one of the judges finally makes the announcement.

"Jack Bradley, please step forward. You're the final contestant to make it through to the next round of Atlanta Idol."

What a relief! I clap my hands together wildly, then reach over to touch Jack's arm as he makes his way to the end of the line of the top fifteen. We beam at each other, our eyes saying more than words ever could.

"Everyone else, we're sorry, but you didn't make it this time. Don't give up. Keep singing and come back next year. Thanks, y'all." The judges wait while the contestants who didn't make it exit the stage.

"Congratulations to y'all who got through! There's another individual round tomorrow, and we'll narrow it down to the top five tomorrow night. Good luck!"

We file off the stage and out of the theater into the lobby. It's like I'm floating on a cloud. I have to call my mama to tell her what's going on. We've been text messaging since I left for the contest, and I talked to her briefly our first night in Atlanta. I want to hear her voice again.

"Well hello there, baby girl!" my mama exclaims when she answers her cell phone.

Outside the theater on Peachtree Street, I glance up at the marquee that prominently displays "Atlanta Idol" in neon lights. I turn the volume on my phone up so I can hear better over the noisy cars passing by.

"Hey, Mama! How are you?"

She yawns loudly. "Just fine, darling. About ready to hit the hay. How's the contest?"

"Amazing! I just made it into the top fifteen! Isn't that something?"

"It sure is! I'm so proud of you, sweet pea. I knew my baby would be the star of the show!"

I can just imagine her smiling and nodding with unwavering confidence in me. My mama is my biggest fan, even though she worries about the music business since that's what took Daddy away from her.

I laugh. "Thank you, but I haven't won yet. We'll have to wait and see."

"Just do your best, and if it's in God's plan for you to win, then you'll win. If not, there's another path for you. Have faith, sweetie." She yawns again.

"Thanks, Mama. I know it's late, so you better get some sleep. Everything okay over there? How's the store?"

"Everything's fine. Don't you worry. The store is hectic. I got there early today to do inventory, and we had customers all day. I've been a busy bee." She pauses for a second. "Now you go on and enjoy your night."

"Okay. Goodnight, Mama. I love you."

"Love you too, baby girl. Give Kat a hug and a kiss for me. Keep in touch, you hear?"

"I will."

After I say goodbye to her and hang up, I turn around to see Jack standing just past the theater entrance typing on his phone. I walk over to him. "Hey. What are you up to?"

"Waiting for you. Brett texted me that he's with Ryder, Kat, and Hanna at a late dinner after the game. They want us to meet up with them."

"Where?"

"Hard Rock Café. We can walk from here. It's only down the road."

I smile at him, running my fingers over my large, spiral curls, checking for frizz. Luckily, the humidity hasn't gotten the best of them yet. Kat spent about two hours on my hair this morning. She's going to school to become a hair stylist. She always did my hair before choir performances, and today was no different. I told her not to go overboard, but she always says, "Big voice, big hair." She told me I'm already a star, but my hair would help me look the part.

"Okay, let's go." I loop my arm through Jack's as we head off to Hard Rock.

I'm wearing one of my favorite dresses. It has a wrap bodice with a black and white graphic pattern, and it falls right at my knees. To accessorize, I added a light brown, wide belt, and my mocha suede cowgirl boots. Jack has his black cowboy boots on under his dark blue jeans to match his black button up shirt.

He glances my way as we walk. "You ain't messing around with them beads."

I chuckle, running my fingers over my black and white, beaded bib necklace. "I got this just last week at my mama's store."

"Tell me more about the store."

I study Jack's face for a second, realizing that he's being sincere. I certainly don't need an invitation to talk more, but I love how he's genuinely interested. "She opened it a couple years after my daddy left. It's called Katherine Olivia Jo's. Her name is Jolene, and Kat's full name is Katherine. She wanted everyone to be part of the store's name. Kat and I help out there a lot, and my granddaddy helps, too. He lives near the store."

Jack nods. "It's nice to have a family business. My parents are insurance agents and have their own agency together."

"What are their names?"

"Sara and Ty." Jack hesitates for a few seconds. "What's your dad's name?"

I keep my eyes focused straight ahead, my jaw clenching and neck tightening. I know I've mentioned my daddy several times to Jack, but now it's getting more intimate. A name is personal. "Doug." I take a deep breath, then release it. "His name's Doug."

"He would have been so proud of you tonight."

I appreciate how sweet Jack is being, but I don't want to talk about my daddy anymore. "Thanks. Do you have any brothers or sisters?" I ask, shifting gears in a hurry.

"Nope. Only child. Kat your only sibling?"

"Yeah."

We continue walking and talking. It's real easy to chew the fat with Jack. When we reach the Hard Rock Café, twenty-five minutes have already gone by, but it doesn't seem like it. The loud music that greets us when we enter the restaurant is a surefire indication that it'll be difficult for me and Jack to keep our conversation going. The place is packed with people and southern rock memorabilia. Jack spots Brett, Ryder, Hanna, and Kat at a dark, wooden table near the Hard Rock store, two seats left at the end. I take the one next to Kat and Jack sits across from me next to Brett. They already ordered before we got there, so Jack and I add two barbecue chicken sandwiches to their order.

"Should we get some apple cobbler?" Ryder asks when we're all finished with our meals.

"It probably can't measure up," Brett responds.

"To what?" Hanna wonders.

Kat and I look at each other and shrug, wondering the same thing as Hanna.

Brett leans in like he's about to tell us a big, important secret. "Jack's mom makes the best apple cobbler in all of Carolina."

Ryder nods. "It's true. Mama Bradley's Apple Blackberry Sonker is legendary."

I gulp down the Coke I just sipped, so I won't spit it out. "Sonker? What's that?" I inquire, barely controlling my laughter.

"It's North Carolina's version of cobbler. Deep-dish. Much better, if you ask me." Jack gives me a knowing look. "Mama's sonkers sell out every week at the farmers' market."

Brett raises his eyebrows, glancing back and forth between me, Kat and Hanna. "People come from near and far just for a taste. You have to try some."

"One bite, and you'll be hooked," Ryder adds.

Kat and Hanna continue talking to Brett and Ryder about the best desserts they've ever tasted.

But I give Jack puppy dog eyes. "I wish I could have some of your mama's cobbler. Too bad we live so far away from each other."

"You could visit, you know. North Carolina ain't Mars." He smiles, his peepers twinkling, but that's probably from all the colorful, vibrant lighting coming from the small stage up front where a local band is finishing their set.

Does he really want me to visit someday? Excitement and fear descend on the pit of my stomach. I haven't driven by myself outside Georgia before or even been on a plane. A trip to Jack's hometown would be an adventure, that's for sure. "I could visit, but will I? That's the question," I respond coyly.

"I guess we'll see." Jack stares directly into my eyes for a few long seconds until we're interrupted.

"Y'all coming?" Hanna asks. She had gotten up along with Kat, Ryder, and Brett, and they're obviously ready to leave.

"I thought we were getting dessert," Jack says in confusion.

Brett shakes his head and snickers. "Nah. We're going to watch movies back at the hotel. You would know that if you hadn't been making goo-goo eyes at each other."

Jack and I hurry to our feet to join the group, ignoring Brett's comment and paying no mind to each other…at least for now.

Six

The boys walk back to the hotel together while us girls go in the car. The drive is so short that we beat the boys back and have a chance to get up to our room before they come over. Hanna's in the bathroom fixing her makeup when I walk in.

"I have to pee," I announce. "Go on. Get."

Hanna slathers on more lip gloss and eyeliner. "Hold on. I'm busy."

"Why are you primping so much?"

"Hell-o. Ryder's hot."

I sit down on the edge of the bathtub. "You like him?"

"Uh-huh," Hanna admits, now brushing her hair.

"We're not going to see these boys again after this week."

"So?"

"So, don't do anything you'll regret."

Hanna turns away from the mirror to face me. "I'm just having fun. No harm in that. Besides, we already kissed at the game."

I widen my eyes in disbelief. "You did?"

"Yeah. He's a great kisser. Have you kissed Jack?"

"No! Absolutely not. Why would I?"

"Because he's adorable, and you've been spending a lot of time with him. Not even one little kiss when y'all made the top fifteen?"

Kat appears in the doorway. "Not everyone is like you, Hanna."

Hanna narrows her eyes at Kat. "What are you getting at?"

"You move quicker with boys. All I'm saying is that you and Ollie are different that way. I don't think she should get involved with Jack, and you shouldn't bother with Ryder either. We're going home soon."

"At least I go for the boys I like. You flirt, but you never do anything about it because you like to string Sutter along and keep him wrapped around your little pinky." Hanna leans back against the sink. "It isn't fair to either of you."

Kat's face is scarlet with anger, but she just waves her hand in dismissal as she strides away. "Y'all do whatever you want."

I reach out, shoving Hanna's leg. "Why'd you do that? You know she doesn't like to talk about her relationship with Sutter."

"If you could even call it a relationship."

"Oh, hush. You're on thin ice now."

Hanna laughs, tossing her hair over her shoulder. "She'll get over it. She should hook up with Brett."

"Would you stop?" I roll my eyes. "No one is hooking up with anyone."

"We'll see," Hanna says, flashing a sneaky grin.

Hanna always gets what she wants when it comes to boys. She has a new boyfriend every week. I like a lot of boys, too, but that's usually as far as it goes. My mama is pretty strict about boys and much too overprotective. I suspect it's because she's a single parent, always trying to play both parts of mama and daddy at once. Maybe that's why Kat's been dating Sutter for so long. He's on mama's approved list. She loves Sutter like he's the son she never had. He lives up the street from us and grew up with Kat. They've been dating since fifth grade. Of course, dating is much different at ten years old as opposed to twenty years old. No one is really sure exactly what their relationship is now, and Kat rarely talks about it. Sutter is always with her and practically worships the ground she walks on, but she never calls him her boyfriend. It confuses me and everyone else who knows them. Hanna gives her a hard time about it a lot, but in her own way, she's just looking out for Kat. I know she only wants Kat to be happy, and we aren't convinced that Sutter makes her happy.

We hear a knock on the door to our room, so I scramble to my feet. "I still have to pee. Go answer the door."

Hanna takes one last look at herself in the mirror before whirling around. "Showtime!" she squeals, giving me a wink and an excited hug before closing the door on her way out.

The muffled voices of the boys greeting Kat and Hanna fill the hallway. I wonder what we're all going to do. Are we really going to watch movies?

Apparently, Hanna has other plans. Will Jack kiss me tonight? I start sweating just thinking about it.

My first kiss didn't really count as a real one. It happened during a game of spin the bottle at a school dance in the eighth grade. It was Hanna's idea to sneak away from the dance to play. A group of us wound up in the library, spinning the bottle in the dark between the shelves of books. When it was my turn, the empty Coke bottle pointed to Jared Davis, a boy I had a huge crush on. I giggled and said, "Oh, we don't really have to." I was so relieved that we were in the dark and no one could see me blushing. But Hanna insisted that we had to kiss. Jared and I leaned toward each other, and I closed my eyes since that's what people do on TV. Time seemed to stand still as I waited for Jared. Finally, I felt his lips on mine. They were warm and soft. I wasn't sure what to do, so I froze for a few seconds before pulling away. That was it. Since then, I've kissed a few other boys from school just for fun. And I made out with Dylan Parker, one of my neighbors who's three years older than me, last summer. He was home from college for a few months, and we messed around several times, but his kisses were too wet and sloppy. *Ick.* And we didn't have much in common except summertime boredom. I've yet to have a "wow-kiss," as Hanna calls them. Maybe because I've never been in love.

"Hey y'all," I greet everyone when I emerge from the bathroom.

Jack, Ryder, and Hanna are on the small couch in front of the flat screen TV, and Kat and Brett are sitting in the two individual chairs around the little table by the door to the balcony.

Our room is a mini suite. Hanna and I used most of our graduation money to pay for this trip. Kat pitched in, too, so we were able to get an upgraded room. I eye the TV to find out what everyone is glued to, and near as I can tell from the bloody face screaming, it's a horror movie. They must have found the free movie channels. I plop down on the couch's armrest, and instantly shield my eyes from the blood and guts on the screen. A few minutes later, Hanna and Ryder go outside to the balcony, Kat steps out to the hall to call Sutter, and Brett leaves to get snacks.

Jack pats the open seat next to him. "You can sit here if you want."

"Okay." I move onto the couch but leave a safe distance between us. "Why is that guy's body in the swamp?" I hold my hand to my face again, watching between my fingers.

"I don't know. The cops are investigating it." Jack stares with a creased brow at the movie. "They think everyone has an infection. It's kind of like *Outbreak*. You seen that?"

"Nope. I don't like scary movies." I try not to look as the movie continues, but it's right there in front of me, and Jack is so into it. I gasp when a little boy and his mother are in danger. "I don't want to watch this anymore."

Jack leans over, touching my knee briefly. "It's okay, Ollie. It's only a movie."

"Oh my gosh!" I yell as the terrifying scene unfolds. I grab Jack's arm, turning away quickly to hide my eyes again.

"Alright. Alright," Jack says, changing the channel. "You can open your eyes now." He glances down at my hand still holding onto his arm and smiles. "You ain't into horror movies. Got it. What else do I need to know?"

"There's a lot you don't know about me, Jack Bradley." Without thinking, I give him a flirty smile, and then the room gets real warm.

Jack matches my silly grin with one of his own and raises his eyebrows. "Oh, yeah?"

"Look who I found causing trouble in the hallway," Brett announces as he saunters through the doorway with Kat at his heels.

"I was just trying to get some ice to chew on from the machine," Kat says in her defense.

Brett shakes his head. "That's a bad habit, young lady." He plunks some food down on the table, peering over his shoulder at me and Jack. "She got ice all over the dagum floor!"

Kat shrugs. "Oops." She narrows her eyes at Brett. "You didn't have to take my phone and say goodbye to Sutter. Now he thinks I'm with you."

"You *are* with me. We just shared ice together. Doesn't that mean anything to you?" Brett clutches his chest, pretending to be offended.

"You know what I mean," Kat responds in a huff, rolling her eyes.

"Who's Sutter anyway?" he asks.

I say, "He's her boyfriend," at the exact same moment Kat says, "Just a boy from home." Poor Sutter.

Jack stands up, moving towards the snacks. "Do you have a boyfriend, Ollie?" He doesn't even look at me but focuses instead on the assortment of candy on the table.

"Not right now," I respond.

Hanna always tells me to say that because it gives the impression that there is possibly someone. She says it keeps boys interested and curious. In reality, I don't have anyone special back home.

"Candy?" Jack asks, not saying anything else about boys.

"Sure. What's there?"

"Milky Way, Starburst, Twizzlers, Caramello—"

"I'll have that," I interrupt. "Caramello is my favorite."

"I'm more of a Snickers guy. I like more than just chocolate and caramel. I need that something extra." Jack hands me the Caramello bar before opening a Snickers bar for himself.

We hang out for a while longer, watching TV, eating candy, and talking. Hanna and Ryder stay out on the balcony the entire time. Kat tries repeatedly to get in touch with Sutter, who apparently shut his phone off after Brett talked to him. Brett tries to be extra nice to Kat, but she still seems upset, pouting in the corner. Eventually, he goes out to get Ryder so the boys can go back to their room for the night.

"Once Ryder gets his paws off Hanna, we can go," he announces when he reenters our room from the balcony.

Jack and I laugh, but Kat just breathes an annoyed sigh. When they come in, we all say our goodbyes.

"Y'all have a good night," Jack says on their way out the door, giving us a small wave. "See you in the morning, Ollie." He flashes his most charming smile, and my heart flutters while my stomach somersaults.

When the door clicks shut, Hanna flops down on the bed with stars in her eyes. "I think I'm in love y'all."

Me too, I think, but I don't say a word.

Seven

The following morning, I turn my computer on to check my email and Twitter. I sit at the table in our room while Kat does my hair for Atlanta Idol. The call time is ten o'clock for rehearsal with a break around noon and a performance around three o'clock. I log into Twitter to see what's going on.

"Jack tweeted me," I tell Kat as a smile creeps across my lips.

@OllieMcKenna We can fly baby fly baby fly ;)

Kat stops curling my hair for a second to look at the screen. "What does that mean?"

"He's talking about the song I'm singing today, 'Wrong Baby Wrong Baby Wrong' by Martina McBride."

"Oh, okay. Clever," she remarks without any enthusiasm. She returns to curling, so I start typing.

@JaxBradley Or let's get a little mud on the tires ;)

Kat glances over my shoulder. "Let me guess. He's singing Brad Paisley's 'Mud on the Tires.'"

I nod, grinning from ear to ear at our flirty, lyrical tweets.

"I'll need a whole mess of butter for all this corn," Kat mutters.

"It isn't corny. It's cute."

"Uh-huh. Sure." She puts the curling iron down, so I turn around to face her.

"Are you still mad about the Sutter and Brett thing? It'll blow over, you know. Sutter never stays angry with you."

"I know. I'm more worried about you," she admits. "I see the way you look at Jack. Just promise me you'll stay focused on the competition. Jack will be out of your life soon, but you have a real shot at a singing career. This contest could open doors for you. You're *so* talented. Don't ruin your chances because you're distracted by a silly boy."

"Jack isn't just a silly boy," I shoot back.

"Ollie. Please. Just promise me, okay?"

I hesitate, averting my eyes from Kat. "Okay," I finally agree.

@OllieMcKenna Rehearsing in my room. Can't wait to get going but not quite ready to leave...

I see Jack's tweet and laugh at his reference to our duet song, "American Honey."

@JaxBradley See u soon.

As much as I want to play this fun little game with him, Kat's words run through my head again. She's right. I have to focus. Today's performance is crucial. I put my headphones in and start my playlist of country songs that always pump me up before a show. A few seconds into Kellie Pickler's "Red High Heels," and I'm ready for everyone to watch me walk out onto that stage and prove any doubts I have or they have wrong baby wrong. I'm ready for this, and I'm going to *win*.

♫

When I enter the theater, I find Jack and wait with him in the lobby to be called in to rehearse our songs. To pass the time, we watch country music videos on YouTube. We're engrossed in Vince Gill's video for his song "Next Big Thing," laughing at all the retro scenes when another contestant approaches us.

I met Carly on the first day of the competition, and we chatted for a bit. She's a twenty-year-old from Alabama and sings jazz pop music but got eliminated yesterday. She told me she'd be sticking around to see the rest of the contest to support the other contestants. Bless her heart.

"Hey, Carly," I greet her as she comes towards us. "How's it going, sweetie?"

She smiles, plopping down right in front of us. "Are y'all online?" she wonders, pointing at Jack's laptop. There's an enthusiastic urgency in her voice.

He nods. "Mmhmm."

"Oh, okay. You've seen yourselves then?" She glances back and forth between both of us. Our blank expressions must give her the hint that we have no idea what she's going on about. "Oh my goodness. Y'all haven't seen it."

"What do you mean?" Jack stares at her curiously.

"The duet y'all sang is on the Atlanta Idol YouTube channel, and it already has over two hundred thousand views! In less than twenty four hours!" She's practically shrieking with excitement, but Jack and I continue to gawk at her, bewildered.

"Are you joking?" I mumble in amazement, shaking my head. This can't be true, can it? Why would so many people watch me and Jack? We're not famous.

Carly grabs my arm. "This isn't a joke! Y'all are a hit!"

Jack snaps out of his state of shock long enough to pull up the video of our duet. "Here it is, Ollie. She's right." He marvels at the screen, his mouth hanging open. "Well, dagum."

I lean over, peering at the website. My eyes quickly land on the big number under the video. "Two hundred one thousand, nine hundred forty eight views," I read aloud in disbelief. "How did all these people find our video?"

"Even though Atlanta Idol is a local thing, it's known all over the country. You know that. Plus, stuff spreads like wildfire on the Internet." Carly pauses for a second, her mouth breaking into a huge smile. "And you two are definitely on fire."

"Unbelievable," I whisper.

Jack pats me on the back. "Well done."

"Thanks. You, too." I glance at him, and we both start laughing. This is surreal!

"Let's look at the comments," he suggests. "There are over a hundred."

Carly stands up and straightens her skirt. "Well, I'll leave y'all to enjoy this together. I just wanted you to know about it." She flashes us a big grin again. "Y'all are something else!"

We thank Carly for letting us know about the video and for being so kind to us. She's just darling. Then, we turn our attention back to our video to read what people are saying about us. I stop Jack before he starts to read anything and tell him that not everyone loves us and that there might be some really mean comments. He assures me that if there are so many views, then there has to be at least some positive feedback, and we'll focus on that. He also points out that constructive criticism can help us, if there is any. I agree as we begin scrolling through the comments.

The way they look at each other is adorable, incredible, ahhhh! Who are these kids???

How are they not famous? They're going to be huge stars!

Their voices mix so well together.

Ollie is gorgeous and Jack is hot. What a beautiful couple!

Jack's voice is good but Ollie's voice gives me chills. This girl should win.

Atlanta Idol is kinda lame but these two can definitely sing.

I don't know if this was the best song choice for Jack but he's cute.

I'm in awe. They're only teenagers. Someone give them a record deal. Now!

Hope they make the finals so we can see more of them! Keep posting their videos!

"They're all talking about us, Jack. I still can't believe it!" I playfully push his shoulder. "Most of these comments are so supportive. They like us!"

"I know. Crazy." Jack hasn't stopped smiling since Carly's news sunk in. "But we have to take these with a grain of salt. They're just the opinions of some." He's always level headed no matter what, good or bad.

"You're right." I touch his arm for a second. "Hey, there's something we haven't done."

"What's that?"

"We didn't watch it."

In all the excitement, it didn't even occur to us to actually watch the video to see ourselves sing together.

Jack grins, leaning back. "You do the honors."

I click play. We watch as our duet comes to life again. I remember looking into Jack's eyes like we're the only two in the room, and I feel the same rush of excitement when the audience cheers. We get to relive such a special performance and share it with people everywhere now, not just those in the theater. I blink back a few tears when the video ends.

Jack closes his laptop. "I don't know if that was the best song choice for Ollie," he teases.

"I know. What an ugly couple," I say, following suit.

We gaze into each other's eyes.

"Horrible."

"Awful."

"They shouldn't sing together ever again."

Jack's face is so close to mine that I can practically feel his touch. I hold my breath, wanting him to kiss me so badly. My heart races in anticipation, and I pray that he'll think I'm a good kisser. His eyes wander down to my lips and slowly sweep back up to my eyes. He inches just a little bit closer. He's going to do it. He's going to kiss me!

"Jack, we're ready for you now." A staff member appears beside us, tapping his foot. "Time to rehearse."

Jack pulls back so fast, immediately scrambling to his feet. "Okay. On my way," he assures the guy. He glances back at me, but his face is different. Something has changed. He has a blank expression with a hint of embarrassment, his usually bright blue eyes dull now. "Bye, Olivia."

I can't help but notice that he used my full name. I never thought I could feel so hurt just hearing my own name. I sit there stunned, watching as he disappears into the theater and wondering what the heck just happened.

Later in the day, I pace in the lobby as I wait to be called to the wings for my performance. There's a lot of hanging around. Kat picked me up just after noon, and we had lunch together. Over grilled cheese sandwiches and Cokes, I told Kat all about the video and how surprised Jack and I were to see such support for us. She was really excited for me, so I chose to leave out the part about the almost-kiss. I know she isn't on board with the whole liking Jack thing, and I didn't want her to lecture me again about staying focused. I want to talk to Hanna about what happened, or what didn't happen, but she's spending the day with Ryder. Kat said they went to the aquarium. I consider texting Hanna, but I don't want to hash this out over a series of short messages. Also, I worry that she'll say something to Ryder about it, and then it'll get back to Jack. I'll have to wait until I can talk to her alone. More waiting.

I notice Jack coming towards me in the lobby, and my thoughts gallop around and around with what to say. Should I act normal? I can pretend everything is fine. Well, it *is* fine, isn't it? Nothing has happened between us romantically, and I'm beginning to think that maybe that's for the best. He practically sprinted away from me earlier. Either he's real shy or he doesn't like me in that way, and it's all just a big misunderstanding. I'm not sure, but I don't want to find out right before my performance.

"Hey," he says, standing before me in light blue jeans, a blue plaid shirt and brown cowboy boots. "You ready?" He smiles at me, his whole face brightening. He appears to be more at ease than he was when he bolted before and certainly seems more comfortable getting ready to hit the stage than he did in that moment with me.

"Hope so," I respond, using the calmest voice I can. Just then I'm called backstage along with two other contestants. "I have to go."

"Alright. Go get 'em," Jack drawls, nodding. "I'll be cheering you on."

"Okay," I respond, wondering if he really means that. Where do we stand? I don't know, but I don't have time to think about it now. I hurry off to get backstage. Feeling a rush of nerves, I stop short and turned around to see Jack still watching me. I raise my eyebrows hopefully. "Pray for me, Jack," I blurt out.

"Yes, ma'am," he calls out, then waves his hand encouragingly. "Go on."

I'm relieved that we still support each other no matter what. On my way to the wings, I decide that my friendship with Jack is more important than anything else. I don't want to lose him this week, even if our friendship fizzles out after the contest. I have to stop thinking about the almost-kiss and run lyrics through my head instead.

After the two other contestants perform, it's finally my turn.

Eight

Sweaty and jittery, I take the stage anyway with my head held high. Smiling politely at the judges, I announce the song I'm singing. My music starts, so I instantly shift into performance mode. The feedback on YouTube has boosted my confidence. I bounce around the stage in my short, black-sequined, strapless dress. The ruffled skirt and bedazzled cowgirl boots add some fun flare to my outfit and to my overall stage presence. I'm having a great time interacting with the audience, encouraging them to clap along with me.

About half my song has already gone by when it takes a turn for the worse. I'm standing at the edge of the stage, peering out into the crowd and happily swaying back and forth to the music when I notice a man sitting about four rows back on the end. He looks just like my daddy with messy, dirty blond hair falling into his eyes and that unmistakable angular jaw covered in patchy stubble. I gasp, glued to the stage and wide-eyed like Bambi caught in headlights. I desperately try to see his face clearer through the near blinding lights, almost tumbling forward.

When it's time to sing the next verse, I mumble the correct lyrics, but I know I'm off key and slightly out of sync with the music. The whole performance is crumbling. Dragging my eyes away from that man, I slowly move to the other side of the stage, wanting nothing more than to pull myself together. I finish the verse and force a smile, pretending that I'm in control, even though I'm shaken by the sight of him. When my eyes land on the contestant section of the audience, what I see helps a little bit. Carly is bobbing her head along to the music a few rows behind Jack, who's also nodding along and staring directly into my eyes. I have to keep going, despite the hitch. I sing as best I can, reluctantly grinning at the irony of the chorus about how you have to get up after you fall. Ending the song strong, I then wait on the X taped to the middle of the stage for the judges' comments.

The first judge leans forward to the microphone to give me his feedback. "I loved it! Your voice was rich and powerful, except for that one mistake. It looked like you got lost for a minute, but you found your way back like a pro. Well done!"

The other comments are similar. They point out where I went wrong, but say that overall, they enjoyed my performance. They call it youthful, exciting, and entertaining. I thank them and scurry off the stage to the sound of the crowd's applause and cheers, breathing a huge sigh of relief when I'm out of the spotlight. One of the stagehands gives me a high five, but I think it's undeserved. I screwed up out there. I broke one of the most important and basic rules of performing: Never let an audience member get under your skin. A few tears escape from my eyes, but I wipe them away in a hurry. I'm so disappointed in myself. But what if he really *is* my daddy? I shake my head. No. Impossible. I need some air. I push the door open and come face to face with Jack.

"You alright?" he asks, his brow creased.

I shrug. "I'm okay, I guess." I pause before deciding that I can trust Jack. I need someone to talk to. "I messed up."

"It happens. Every dog has a few fleas. Don't worry about it."

"I know mistakes happen, but it's why this one happened that has me so darn upset." I dab my eye with the back of my hand before any more tears can escape.

Jack tilts his head. "Hey, don't cry. What happened?"

I attempt to maintain eye contact with him, even though I'm embarrassed and still trembling from the incident. "You'll think it's stupid."

"No, I won't."

"Okay, well," I start, taking a deep breath, "I saw someone in the audience who looked just like my daddy, and it threw me for a loop. It couldn't really be him, though. Could it?"

"It's unlikely, unless somehow he knows that you're in this competition."

"I doubt he knows anything about me," I reply, my voice low and wrought with bitterness.

Jack's face falls before he glances down. "Sorry, Ollie. It's tough. But you were great, anyway," he tries to convince me, raising his eyes to mine again. "And you look real pretty."

I can't help but go red. "Well, thank you."

The door flies open, and a stagehand appears there in a frazzled state, clipboard in hand and headset covering his ears. "There you are, Jack. You're up next." He presses a button and speaks into his tiny microphone. "Found him. He's en route to the stage."

"What are you doing wasting time talking to me when you have to sing any minute?" I feel so foolish telling him my problems when he's just trying to get backstage.

"Talking to you is never a waste of my time." And with that, he breezes past me through the door to go get set.

I'm glad Jack is already inside so he can't see me blushing. *Again.* He's the sweetest boy I've ever met. Now, when I count my blessings, I count Jack.

Jack sings "Mud on the Tires" flawlessly. He knocks it out of the park. I'm so happy for him and so relieved that I didn't distract him with our conversation. When he sings, it's effortless. He has such a gorgeous, pure tone that gives me chill bumps. Jack is the last contestant to sing before we get a break. Then, I have a chance to hang out with Kat outside. I share why I botched my performance, and she dismisses the whole thing as ridiculous.

"There's no way Daddy was in there," she asserts, typing on her cell phone, probably to Sutter. When she's finished, she shoves it in her pocket and meets my worried eyes. "Don't even give it another thought."

"But I ruined my song," I whine, still sulking.

Kat shakes her head. "That's simply not true. Don't be so hard on yourself. You sang amazingly well as always, and I was so impressed with how quickly you got right back into it. You didn't miss a beat. You should be proud of yourself." She smiles, and leans in, giving my arm a gentle squeeze. "You're stunning in that dress, and your hair is gorgeous, if I do say so myself."

"Thanks," I reply meekly, barely hearing all her compliments.

"Don't get rattled by people in the audience. You're better than that."

Easier said than done, I think. But instead, I mutter, "Yeah, lesson learned."

"Good."

Kat hasn't seen that guy and his uncanny similarities to our daddy, but I decide to drop it since she isn't having any of it. I certainly can't talk about this with my mama, and Hanna isn't around much lately, so I have to try to let it go and move on.

The break goes on longer than it's supposed to because the judges are deciding on the top five. We wait and wait and wait. Kat stays with me the whole time, keeping me company. I listen to music while she texts Sutter. I don't even bother asking what's going on between them. Kat and I stay outside most of the time while Jack is inside with Brett and some of the other contestants. I want to go in and socialize, but when I mention that Brett showed up, Kat makes the most disgusted face. I assume she's still annoyed about what he did the night before, but I actually think he's a nice guy and try to convince her of that. Unfortunately, she isn't buying any of what I'm selling.

I pull my phone out of my bag and see a text message from Jack.

Judges r takin so long! Just want 2 know either way…

He read my mind. I start typing my reply.

Me too! Tired of waitin… sooo bored & anxious…

A few seconds after I hit send, I notice a new text message alert. He has written back already.

Why don't u come in here? We can check YouTube ;)

I'm about to write again and tell him that Kat is being stubborn when one of the staff members comes outside to get me. It's time for the results. I head back into the theater and onto the stage with the other fourteen contestants. We're told where to stand. Jack is on the other side of the line as far from me as possible. I don't know what that means, if anything. I stand there, praying to God that I make it through, then I glance over at Jack. He's staring straight ahead expressionless, his hands in his pockets and his body stiff, waiting for the news. He doesn't show his nerves, but I know he's as anxious as I must look.

Before I know it, three contestants have made it into the top five. There are only two spots left. I brace myself for the inevitable and remind myself that no matter what happens, it's God's plan. I also remind myself to breath. Jack's name is called. A sense of relief for him surges through my body mixed with even more anxiety because now there's only one more spot left. In that moment, I silently tell God that I'm ready for this and beg Him for a chance to prove it. Beads of sweat trickle down my back. As the seconds tick by at an agonizingly slow rate, my body heats up. If they don't announce who gets the final spot soon, I'll need to sit down and have a glass of water. I don't know how much more of this suspense I can take. Is it really as long as it seems?

I continue to repeat, "Please, please, please," in my head with my eyes tightly shut. When I finish praying, one of the judges clears his throat.

"As you well know, we can only accept one more contestant into the semi-finals. And that person is…"

I hold my breath and force my eyes open, staring pleadingly at the judges. From my peripheral vision, I can tell that Jack is watching me, but I refuse to look at him. If I don't make it through, the devastation will be too much to bare, and the last thing I want is to see pity in his eyes.

"The fifth finalist is…" the judge starts again. Why is this man determined to torture us?

I want to scream at him to say the darn name already. Then, my growing frustration is instantly replaced with sweet relief and overwhelming joy. I have never been so elated to hear, "Olivia McKenna," ever in my life before, so much so that I burst into tears. Funny how my full name can elicit such happiness and sadness within me, all depending on who is saying it.

Nine

After the top five contestants are announced, I'm whisked off to take pictures and do interviews for the local news. Several interviewers ask me how it feels to be in the top five of Atlanta Idol. What a ridiculous question. Then, I think of that old saying, "There aren't any stupid questions, just stupid people." But my mama would be so ashamed if I ever said anything like that out loud. Instead, I smile politely and give them the obvious answer. It feels amazing! I'm plum thrilled and can't wait to see where this journey takes me next. The five of us are cheesin' for the cameras and loving every minute of the attention.

When we're done with the press, Kat and I head back to our hotel room. We're both exhausted, so we order room service and watch movies. Hanna comes back to the room eventually and declares that she's head over heels for Ryder. She had the best day of her life. So did I, and I'm disappointed that our best days didn't include each other. Kat and Hanna fall asleep around eleven o'clock, but I lay awake, much too excited to even close my eyes. I can't believe I made the top five! I'm beyond grateful and have to do something with my nervous energy. I text Jack.

Can't sleep.

About a minute later, he responds.

On the roof. Come up.

I glance over at Kat and Hanna who are sleeping soundly and decide not to wake them. I quietly put my sneakers on and slip out the door.

When I get to the rooftop pool in my bright pink and black, starry pajama bottoms and my Betty Boop t-shirt, I hear familiar music. There are only a handful of people there, and I immediately spot Jack on the other side of the deck. He's sitting by himself wearing sweatpants and a blue Tar Heel t-shirt, strumming his guitar.

As I approach him, he greets me with his eyes first. "Hey. Have a seat."

I sit down next to him on the lounge chair. "I didn't know you play guitar. It sounded really good."

"Thanks," he responds, nodding. "I do alright." He pauses, giving me a curious look. "You play?"

"Nope. But I'd love to learn someday."

"Looks like someday is today," Jack says, pulling the strap over his head. He holds the guitar out to me. "Here."

I take it, even though I'm unsure of what to do.

"Okay, put your fingers like this," he instructs me, positioning them on the neck of the guitar. "I was playing 'American Honey' when you came up."

"You know how to play that?" I ask, surprised. "Why didn't you play live when we sang it?"

Jack shrugs. "Thought it would be better to just go with the track." He gestures to the guitar. "Standard tuning is E, A, D, G, B, E. But the tuning for 'American Honey' is much different." He leans over and strums the beginning of the song. "It starts with a simple riff, and there are only about five chords in the whole song."

I raise my eyebrows. "Okay… Are you sure this is a good place to start for a beginner?"

"You can do it."

"Why don't you play it for me so I can hear how it sounds?"

Jack agrees, taking the guitar back from me. He begins to play the beautiful melody, and I'm lost in his music. We sing together again just like we had before. It's so relaxing this time. It simply feels good to sing with Jack without any judges watching. So natural. So comfortable.

When we finish the song, there are a few cheers from the people in the pool. I smile at Jack. "Play something else."

"Like what?"

"Do you write your own stuff?"

He hesitates for a few seconds. "Uh… yeah."

"I want a Jack Bradley original," I press. "Go on."

"I don't know. Don't really sing my own songs for anyone…"

I put my hand on his forearm and stare at him until he has no choice but to meet my eyes. "I'm not just anyone."

Jack hems and haws for a few more minutes until I finally convince him to play just the first verse. "Alright. Alright. It's called Carolina Blue." He points his finger at me. "Just the first verse. And no laughing at me."

I raise both my hands. "Promise."

When he begins to play, I forget about everything else around us. In that moment, nothing else exists. No people in the pool. No sticky Georgia heat. No sounds from the hustle and bustle on the streets below. Just me, Jack, and his guitar. He doesn't stop after the first verse either. He sings that whole song right to me. As I listen to the words that Jack wrote, I can't help but wish I was the girl he wrote them about. His musical talent and creativity inspire me. He has the ability to draw me into the song and make me pay attention. I *have* to write songs with Jack.

Carolina Blue
Written by Jack Bradley

Heading to the game
All decked out in that Tar Heel blue
Showing the spirit
Showing the pride
It's good to be on the Carolina side

I saw her in the stands looking real pretty
Daisy Dukes and cowboy boots
Blue flower in her golden hair
Made my way over
And got to talking

I said, "Hey darlin'. How ya doing?
Your eyes are my favorite shade of blue."
She said, "Nice try, but I know better
than to fall for a sweet talker like you."

Hanging with the boys
Sipping sweet tea after a win
Talking stats and scores over fried chicken
Couldn't ask for much more
Until she breezed through the door

I said, "Hey darlin'. How ya doing?
Your eyes are my favorite shade of blue."
She said, "Nice try, but I know better
than to fall for a sweet talker like you."

Trying anyway
Hoping she'd look my way
Not giving up just yet
Fight, fight, fight for Carolina

I said, "Hey darlin'. How ya doing?
Your eyes are my favorite shade of blue."
She took my hand and said, "It's hard to resist
a charming boy like you."

I gazed into her eyes, mesmerized
Bright as the sky on a clear day
And I couldn't resist that Carolina blue.

Ten

Rehearsals are in full swing the next day. I'm fixing to put on quite a show the following day with the other four contestants. This is when the competition gets even more serious. Tickets for the top five showcase are sold out. Each contestant will sing two individual songs, a duet or trio number, and two group numbers with all five contestants. Needless to say, I'm shaking in my boots.

The producers chose me and Jack to sing the duet and the remaining three contestants to sing as a trio. We all have to learn some basic choreography for the group songs, too. My head is spinning with lyrics, melodies, cues, and dance moves. As if that isn't enough, this is the round when audience voting begins. The people in the theater will vote from their seats for individual contestants, and the individual performances will be streamed live to Atlanta Idol's website for online votes. When all the votes are counted, the top two vote getters will go to the final round. I barely have a minute to wrap my head around all the people who will see me sing and vote for me. Or not vote for me. It's exciting and absolutely terrifying.

At the end of a grueling day jam packed with individual rehearsals and group rehearsals, Jack and I venture back to the hotel to rehearse our duet. We go through both of our iTunes playlists and can't decide between singing "I Got You" by Thompson Square or "Don't You Wanna Stay" by Jason Aldean and Kelly Clarkson. They are two completely different sounds.

"'I Got You' is more upbeat than 'American Honey,' so that could be a good direction to go in," I point out to Jack. I'm standing near the microwave in the kitchenette in Jack's hotel room while he's perched on the counter with his laptop.

He takes a sip of his Coke. "True. 'Don't You Wanna Stay' is much more powerful, but I'm not too sure about it."

"Why?"

"It's real intense, and we might get docked for not being youthful or something like that. People might not relate to us singing that type of song." He shrugs, fixing his eyes on his laptop again.

I nod, taking my water out of the microwave. My throat is scratchy, so I'm drinking lots of tea and water. "It's popular across genres, though. If people recognize it, they might connect to it more." I sigh, dipping the teabag in and out of my mug. "I don't know, Jack, but I do know that I'm tired."

"Me, too, but we gotta choose a song and get going."

"If we can pull off 'Don't You Wanna Stay,' I think it would get us through to the finals."

Jack creases his brow, staring up at the ceiling. He leans back and stretches his legs out.

"You have long legs," I observe. "How tall are you?"

"About five eleven," he responds, smiling at me. "Get up here, you." He pats the counter next to him. "Let's watch performances of both songs to get a feel for 'em."

I set my tea down and take Jack's hand, so he can help me hop up on to the counter. I don't really need any assistance, but I do want to hold his hand, if only for a few seconds.

We watch several different videos of the same two songs. They're both real dynamic in a live setting. Crowds clap along to "I Got You," but they give standing ovations for "Don't You Wanna Stay."

I push Jack's shoulder with mine. "Well, what do you think?" I bury my face in my hands. "I'm still not sure," I groan.

"Only one thing to do," he announces.

"What's that?"

"We'll sing them both. Right now. Whichever sounds better and feels better is the one we'll choose." He holds out his fist, so I hit it with mine.

"Yeah, we really just did a fist bump." I start laughing.

Jack glances at me, chuckling, too. "I'm so exhausted, Ollie," he whines in between laughs, leaning on me. "I'll tell ya that."

"Maybe we should have some coffee or something. I think there's some in there," I say, pointing to the cupboard on the other side of the counter. "I've gotta keep drinking as much as I can anyway."

Jack gives me a puzzled look. "Why?"

"My throat feels funny. It hurts just a little bit."

"You sure you want to keep going tonight?"

"I'm fine," I lie, trying to swallow without wincing. I can't tell if my throat is just dry and worn out from singing or if I'm coming down with something. "Come on. Let's sing."

Jack pulls up the lyrics and music for both songs. We try "I Got You" first, and it's a fun tune with a really positive, upbeat feel about two people needing each other and sticking side by side. Then it's "Don't You Wanna Stay." The combination of the honest lyrics about love, the violin, and the melancholic guitar riffs is incredibly powerful and mesmerizing. Jack and I are drawn into the torturous emotions conveyed by the words, music, and our voices, and I'm certain the song will have the same effect on an audience. We're so into it that by the end, we barely realize someone is knocking at the door.

I stare into Jack's eyes, still in a daze and fighting back tears. Our voices blended astonishingly well together. The knocking gets louder.

"I think someone's at the door. Maybe Brett and Ryder are back from the pool with Kat and Hanna." I'm saying words, but my head and my heart remain in that song. I'm struggling to pull away from it.

Jack finally tears his eyes away from mine. "Yeah. Right. Probably them," he mumbles absentmindedly as he jumps off the counter and heads for the door.

I hear a strange man's voice speaking to Jack, then he responds with, "Okay. I'm sorry about that, sir. I understand." When he gets back to the kitchenette, I ask him who it was.

"It was the guy in the next room. He said we're being too loud."

"Oh," I reply. "But did he at least like what he heard?"

We look at each other seriously for a second before doubling over with laughter.

"Shhh," Jack whispers, still grinning. "Or he'll come back. Don't get us kicked out." He hoists himself up onto the counter next to me again and opens his laptop. "Back to work. Which song?"

I drink some of my tea to calm down after my giggle fit. "I know which one I want."

"Okay. On the count of three, we both say what we want. One…two…three!"

"'Don't You Wanna Stay,'" Jack and I say together.

He throws his arm up in the air in triumph. "Nice!"

"Have you ever acted?" I wonder. "We'll need to do a little bit of that to make this believable."

"I was in a few school plays."

"Me too. We have to pretend that we want to stay with each other, but we have to say goodbye. That's pretty much the song, you know."

"And that's pretty much us." He shifts his body away from me. "Uh, I mean because we have to say goodbye in a couple days." He jumps off the counter and holds his hand out for me. "Come on. Let's rehearse a few more times before we call it a night."

"Where? That guy already has his panties in a twist." I grab Jack's hand and hop down.

"I don't know. My truck?"

"Sure. Lead the way." I take a few more sips of my tea and grab a bottle of water from the refrigerator.

"I've got your jacket. Don't forget your bag," Jack reminds me, holding the door open.

I gather all my stuff together before heading to his truck. We rehearse the song a few times in the parking lot. Singing in parking lots is becoming our thing. It's fun, though. The dimly lit parking garage sets the mood for our ballad. We work hard on it until my voice is shot, and Jack is worn out. He walks me back to my room, giving me a hug in front of the door. It seems sort of date-like, but I tell myself that it's just rehearsal and good manners.

"Goodnight, darlin,'" he drawls as he releases me from our embrace. He gives me another sweet smile, then takes off down the hall.

"Night," I mumble after him, watching him walk toward the elevators. I can't take my eyes off his long, lean legs in those tight blue jeans and the way his fitted black t-shirt clings to his upper body and shows off his tan, toned arms. I force myself to look away when he turns the corner, but there's no denying how attractive he is. Jack is sexy in an all-American boy kind of way.

I open the door and find Kat and Hanna watching TV. "Hey, y'all."

"It's about time, missy," Hanna says, tapping her wrist, even though she isn't wearing a watch. "You're way past curfew." She guffaws and gets up to give me a hug.

"Missed you today," I confess.

"I missed you, too!"

"How was your day with Ryder? Are y'all getting hitched?" It's my turn to cackle.

"Laugh it up. But maybe someday. He's so cool. I love spending time with him." Her face glows with happiness.

I don't remember a time that I've seen her like this. Maybe it's more serious than I think. But we just met these boys.

"Okay," I say simply. I'm too tired to get into it with her. I need some sleep. My throat is all prickly and dried out. I unzip my luggage to get my pajamas out.

"I'm going to sleep, y'all," Kat announces from the other side of the room. "Oh, Ollie, I checked YouTube, and your video is past five hundred thousand views now."

I jerk my head up to survey Kat's face. No signs of fibbing. I quickly realize that she's serious. Suddenly, I'm frozen, holding my makeup remover in one hand and toothbrush in the other. I keep having the same thoughts over and over again. *Who is viewing our video so many times?* And more importantly, *why are they watching it?* Maybe Jack and I do have something special.

Eleven

The morning of the top five showcase is hectic, to say the least. I'm up at six o'clock for hair and makeup with Kat. When we finish, I get dressed and dash right over to Jack's room to rehearse our duet a few more times before heading to late morning group rehearsals. The show is set for seven o'clock that night, and the nervous energy is already pulsing through my body. Jack is good at distracting me from it, though. He pulls up games and songs on his phone to show me and tells me the most ridiculous jokes. I laugh at each one, even when they aren't funny. He's being so considerate. My throat still isn't quite right from the night before, so Jack makes sure I have lozenges and tea with me at all times. He even made a honey, lemon tea for me that his mama used to make for him when he was younger.

After group rehearsals, we have some downtime, so I read and re-read the lyrics for my two solos. I'm fixing to sing Miranda Lambert's "The House That Built Me" and Pam Tillis's "When You Walk In the Room." Instead of singing the songs, I quietly hum the melodies while reading the lyrics, trying my best to save my voice for later. To avoid talking, I send an email to my mama to tell her about the YouTube video and to give her the details of the top five showcase. I know she isn't coming, but I want her to feel like she's involved. It also makes me feel like she's part of it. I really wish she were here. She would be the best person to make sure I have the right outfits. My mama's style is beautiful and unique. I adore everything she wears and love getting my clothes from her store. The dresses I brought with me are from there, but I still want my mama here to see me in them and help me accessorize. I'm really lucky to at least have Kat with me since she's a piece of my mama.

In no time, it's late afternoon, and seven o' clock is quickly approaching. I pace backstage in my frothy, organza corset dress and my shimmery gold, peep toe pumps. Kat and Hanna told me over and over again how beautiful I look before they went into the theater to find their seats. I observe myself in the brightly lit mirror, wondering if I should wear my cowgirl boots instead of heels. My long, loose curls flow over my shoulders and onto my dress like I'm a country princess in a Dixie fairytale. I take a deep breath, reveling in the moment. I'm actually here in the semi-finals of Atlanta Idol.

"There's my baby!"

I see my mama in the mirror rushing up behind me. I whirl around in surprise, practically tripping on my own two feet when I hear that familiar voice. "Mama!" I squeal. "What in the world are you doing here?"

"You didn't think I'd miss my baby in the semi-finals, did you?" She squeezes me tightly before pulling back to examine my face. "How are you doing? Kat told me you have a sore throat. Oh, my poor little girl. Did you take any medicine? Want me to get you some water? What do you need, baby? Tell me. I'm here now." She's talking so fast, I can barely keep up.

"Slow down, Mama. I'm fine. Trying to rest my voice until show time." I nod, giving her a small smile. "Don't worry."

"Okay. Just let me know. I've got my cell phone." She surveys the area. "Where's Kat?"

"In the theater with Hanna."

"Alright. I'll go find her and get out of your hair, which looks gorgeous, by the way. You look stunning. This dress fits you like a glove. I knew it would! You look so grown up. I'm so proud of you!" Her eyes well with tears as she stands back, admiring me. "My baby," she whispers.

"Thanks, Mama," I murmur, hugging her tightly again. I hold back my tears since I don't want to ruin my makeup.

My mama arrived like a bull in a China shop, but I'm so happy to have her here. She's so full of life and encouragement, which is exactly what I need. After she leaves my dressing room, I breathe much easier compared to when I first got to Atlanta. I know I'll be fine tonight, despite my sore throat and my nerves. I always sing better when my mama is in the audience.

♫

One of the stage managers appears in the doorway. "We're ready for you, Ollie."

"Okay. Thank you," I reply, wringing my hands together.

It's time to sing, "The House That Built Me." I've practiced and practiced, so the only thing left to do now is get out there and do my best. I inhale deeply, then exhale slowly before walking into the hallway to head to the stage. This song always makes me emotional, especially now that I've been away from home, but I pray that I can channel my feelings into my performance rather than let them take over.

At the side of the stage, I wait for my cue from the show's host for the evening.

"Next up is a real extraordinary young woman with a big ol' voice singing a song made popular by Miranda Lambert. Please give a warm Atlanta Idol welcome to Miss Olivia McKenna!"

I step in front of the wildly applauding crowd and thank the host before he departs, leaving me alone under the spotlight. Flashing my pearly whites, I remove the microphone from the stand as the music floods the room. I hear a loud whistle and then, "That's my baby!" in an unmistakable voice. My body relaxes, and I launch into the song.

The show is going off without a hitch. I make it through both of my solos without any major problems, and hurry backstage to the dressing room to change for my duet with Jack. My voice is raspier than usual, but it actually adds some unique layering to my sound. My throat is still hurting, but I'm pushing through, anyway. I slip into an emerald dress with ornate lace overlain on a pale, tan lining, ruching on the neckline, and a tie sash. There's a knock at the door when I'm putting my onyx gold earrings on.

"Come on in."

Jack stands in the doorway. "Ready?" He's devilishly handsome in a black blazer over a forest green, collared shirt tucked into his dark blue jeans with a black leather belt and shiny, new, black boots.

"Do these earrings look alright?" I ask absentmindedly, staring at myself in the mirror.

"You look perfect," he says, reddening slightly when I glance at him. "Let's go."

"Wait. Do we have time to sing the chorus? I'll feel better if we do it one more time."

Jack steps into the room and closes the door behind him. "Yeah, but we gotta hurry. On three. One…two…three."

We both start singing in unison. I get the same rush of excitement I always do when I sing with Jack, or whenever I stare into his eyes.

"That sounded good," I tell him after we finish the chorus.

He agrees, taking my hand as we walk toward the stage. We say a quick prayer while we wait to go on. The duet is staged so that he walks out before me for the first verse, and then I join him for the chorus.

We hear the host say, "Ladies and gentleman, it's the duo you've been anxiously awaiting! Their duet

"American Honey," has been sweeping the Internet since they sang it on this very stage. Now, singing "Don't You Wanna Stay," please welcome Jack Bradley and Olivia McKenna!"

The theater erupts into deafening applause and cheers, everyone bursting with excitement for us. The amount of enthusiasm is thrilling, yet still mindboggling.

I pat Jack's back right before he goes out to face the crowd. "Sell it, baby."

He turns around, shaking his head a bit as his mouth slowly curls up into a playful grin.

"Go get 'em!" I watch him command the stage and start our song, adjusting my in-ear monitor and gripping the microphone tightly with my clammy hands as I inch closer to my debut.

When I make my entrance, the audience claps like crazy. I'm taken by surprise for a second, but don't miss a beat. Our duet is even better than the first one. As I sing with Jack, feeding off his energy and the liveliness of the crowd, I'm sure I can get used to this. In fact, I already am. I love every second I spend with Jack.

After the show ends, the five of us wait onstage for the audience voting to be counted and the online voting to close. It seems like the anticipation goes on forever, but finally the results are ready. We all hold hands tightly, our heads down, awaiting our fates. My heart is pounding so hard I can feel it in my throat and hear it in my ears. The theater falls silent for the judges to read off the final two names. Within seconds, the crowd roars with applause. I feel like I'm having an out of body experience. I see Jack's eyes dart rapidly in downright shock right before I burst into tears. He swiftly enfolds me into his arms. The other contestants rally around us. I can barely hear what they're saying over the big hullabaloo in the theater.

Jack and I are the final two.

We're quickly whisked away again to do some local press. Photographers snap pictures, and journalists question us. After the last interview, we have a moment to breathe.

"Dagum," Jack mutters.

"Oh my goodness," I whisper.

We stare at each other, shaking our heads, smiles creeping across our faces.

"Excuse me. Jack? Olivia?" A middle-aged man with sand colored hair appears next to us, anxiously waiting to speak to us. I assume he's another interviewer. We nod for him to continue. "I'm Will Kirk and this is my wife, Alyssa," he informs us, pointing to a petite dark-haired woman standing slightly behind him.

She steps forward. "We're from Kirk Entertainment." She holds her hand out to me.

I embrace it, smiling sweetly. "Nice to meet you both," I say, shaking Will's hand next.

Jack shakes their hands, too. "Yeah, good to meet you, sir, ma'am. Is this for another interview?" he wonders.

Will and Alyssa glance at each other for a second.

"No," Alyssa responds. "We're managers in the music industry."

"We're based in Nashville," Will continues, "and we'd like to represent both of you together. As a duo."

Twelve

Gazing at Atlanta from the balcony of our hotel room real early the next morning, I sip sweet tea, enjoying the fresh air and the peaceful moment that's sure to pass quickly. The final show is tonight, and I'm seeking a way to calm my nerves. Kat and Mama are still asleep, but they'll be up soon, and the finale chaos will begin. My thoughts keep wandering back to Will and Alyssa. Last night, Jack and I thanked them for their interest in us and took their card, but we voiced our skepticism to each other once they were out of ear-shot. Everything is happening so fast, and we're so busy that we don't know which way to turn. Do we want to be a duo? I haven't ever considered joining a duo or a group. I've always been sure that I would pursue my music career on my own. But the more I think about being in a duo with Jack, the more I like the idea. Our duets sound great, and we get along pretty well. Maybe it makes the most sense to do this together.

"Ollie!" Kat calls from inside. "Get in here. Time to get your hair done." She's up and raring to go. Ready or not, I have to be, too.

Kat styles my hair high above my forehead and pulls my long, wavy hair back into a ponytail, convincing me that it looks sophisticated and finale worthy. She gives me a pair of large hoop earrings to complement my up-do. After my hair is done, my mama shows me five dresses that she brought with her. I choose three of them, one for each song I'll sing in the final show.

My ailing throat persists, but I rehearse for most of the day, taking frequent breaks to drink tea and rest my voice. There aren't any duets planned for the finale, just three individual performances each from me and Jack. I'm relieved about that since it takes some of the pressure off, but I haven't seen Jack all day. I figure he's rehearsing his songs, too. But I also wonder if he's thinking about what Will and Alyssa said to us. Is he seriously considering partnering up with me to try to get a record deal? I want to talk to him about it some more, but don't want to lose my focus on the task at hand: the final performances.

After rehearsals, the last show of the competition is a blur of excitement, anticipation, anxiety, and the list goes on. So many emotions whirl around inside me as I take the stage three different times. Mama says my first dress looks like sweet blueberry iced tea. It's a navy hued sleeveless, scoop neck dress with a ruched top and floral cutout skirt overlay. It's certainly no coincidence that I'm wearing it to sing "Blue" by LeAnn Rimes.

Immediately after exiting the stage, I hurry to my dressing room to change into my next outfit. By this point, Jack and I have only exchanged a few words in passing and said a prayer before the show started. It's an intense situation, to say the least. My mama accompanies me to the dressing room where she helps me into a ruffled, single shoulder dress. She comments that the coral color of this flowing dress and my blue eyes make me look like a beautiful day at the beach. I study myself in the mirror, admiring my relaxed yet glamorous ensemble. Taking a deep breath, I follow my mama backstage to get set to sing Deana Carter's "Strawberry Wine." The show is sold-out, and the crowd is fantastic, cheering each time I walk onstage and giving standing ovations after my songs.

Minutes after my second performance, I rush to the dressing room with my mama again. We're getting the hang of it by this point. Get dressed, sing, change clothes, sing again. My final song is "Anyway" by Martina McBride. I slip into my last ensemble, a strapless dress adorned with a cascading waterfall ruffle along its front. The smooth, woven, golden yellow fabric shimmers, which will be perfect under the bright lights. The bowed sash belt is a sweet accent to the flirty, full skirt. I absolutely adore this dress. It's my favorite by far.

I arrive backstage as Jack is exiting. I didn't see any of his performances because I was changing outfits while he was singing. He wore the same dark jeans, white button up shirt, and navy blue blazer for all his performances. Boys always have it so much easier when it comes to fashion. Jack doesn't have to worry about shoes or accessories. He always wears his cowboy boots and cross necklace.

"Hi, darlin,'" Jack greets me with a smile and a nod. "You're a sight for sore eyes."

"Hey. How'd you do out there?"

"Can't complain."

"Good." I breathe in deeply. "Okay, gotta go. Pray for me." I turn on my heel to head to the stage and practically lose my balance on my four-inch peep toe pumps.

"Hey, Ollie," Jack calls after me.

Carefully, I swivel back around, putting my arms out to steady myself.

"Have fun." He flashes a quick smile at me before disappearing out the door.

My mama rushes over to me, wrapping me up in a tight hug and almost knocking me off my feet again. "Good luck, baby. Or break a leg or whatever y'all performers say."

I thank her, but still feeling wobbly, I also pray that the old theater expression won't actually come true.

"Love you!" she shouts as I saunter onstage to the sound of earsplitting applause.

Here we go, I think. No matter what happens, I have to do my best. Even if no one likes it, my voice sounds too raspy, and I don't win, I still have to try. I have to sing it, anyway.

Back onstage after a thirty-minute intermission, Jack and I wait to hear the results. The audience votes were counted, and the online voting was closed. Everything has been added up and a winner has been chosen. Who is it? Jack puts his arm around my waist and I hold onto him tightly, too. I'm shaking from head to toe in anticipation. The results can change my life forever. The seconds tick by, seeming like hours. All the judges stand alongside us onstage. The head judge finally steps forward, holding a blue envelope in his hand. He speaks to the crowd for a few minutes, going over the prize money that both of us will receive and recapping our performances. Tiny beads of sweat trickle down my back and form on my forehead. I can't take much more, and I'm tempted to lunge forward and rip the envelope out of his hands. I *have* to know the results. Jack glances my way, and we smile at each other when we lock eyes.

"And the winner of Atlanta Idol is…"

A drum roll pounds through the speakers, filling the judge's dramatic pause. I hold my breath, staring at my shoes as my heart gallops ahead like a horse in the Kentucky Derby. Jack and I cling to each other through what seems like the longest pause in history. I finally breathe out slowly, bracing myself for the big reveal.

"Jack Bradley!"

The audience explodes with excitement, rising to their feet to cheer the winner on. Jack bends over in shock while I remain frozen for a second, too stunned to move. Then, I remember to smile and pat Jack on the back. He stands up straight, his eyes glassy from tears. All it takes is one look into his watery, blue eyes and I lose it, bawling like a baby as Jack scoops me up into a hug. I cry happy tears for Jack winning and for me coming in second and disappointed tears for Jack winning and for me coming in second. I'm so glad that I got so far in the competition, but second place still stings. I came to Atlanta to win.

Once we exit the stage, our families and friends greet us backstage. Jack's parents flew in this morning to see him compete in the final round. He bolts over to them, joining them and Brett and Ryder in a group hug. I walk over to my mama, Kat, and Hanna.

"Hey y'all," I say flatly, trying to muster up a smile.

"There's our star!" my mama shouts. "Well done, sweetie. Well done." She puts her arm around me and kisses the top of my head.

I rest my head on her shoulder and cry into her shirt. "I wanted to win, Mama. I wanted this so bad."

"I know, baby girl. I know." She strokes my hair gently. "You're always a winner in my eyes."

"Getting this far out of thousands is pretty incredible," Hanna chimes in, placing her hand on my shoulder. "You did it!"

Kat puts her arm around me, too. "This is just a stepping stone. Take this and move forward. You're destined to be a singer one way or another."

I nod, feeling better just knowing they're always by my side. "Thanks, y'all."

"Let's go to dinner to celebrate after you do press," Hanna suggests.

"Good idea!" my mama approves.

"We'd like to join you," Alyssa says, appearing behind my mama with Will. "We really enjoyed the show and would love to continue our conversation with you and Jack over dinner." She says it loud enough for Jack and his group to hear, too.

Jack glances our way. We both shrug.

"I'm up for it if you are," he agrees, making eye contact with me.

My mama, Kat, and Hanna are nodding and smiling at me, so I know they're fine with it, too.

"Okay. Sure," I respond finally. "Thank you."

"Great!" Will exclaims. "How about we meet in an hour or so at Murphy's? It's just a few miles from here. Our treat."

Thirteen

Jack and I do more interviews with the local news after making our dinner plans. Most of the reporters are nice, but some are so pushy.

"Y'all seem to get along so well. What's going on here?" This particular reporter stares at us with his beady little eyes, waiting for some kind of gossip.

"Uh, we both love to sing. We've become friends, and we enjoy singing together. That's all," Jack answers.

"Y'all aren't dating?" he presses on, his shiny, bald head wet from sweat.

Jack lets out a hearty laugh. "Ain't no time for none of that. We've been working hard."

"I'm happy for Jack, and he's happy for me. We support each other, and that's all there is to it. Thank you." I grab Jack's arm and whisk him away with me to the next reporter, leaving the beady-eyed, bald man in the dust with his mouth hanging open. He's probably still curious about us. I laugh to myself and think, *No harm in letting him wonder.*

Jack and I arrive at the restaurant to meet up with everyone else about an hour later, as planned. We look around and spot my mama, Jack's parents, Kat, Hanna, Brett, and Ryder at a long table with Alyssa and Will. My mama sees us and waves us over. Once we greet everyone, we sit down to order.

"What are you getting?" I ask Jack, opening my menu.

He's already perusing the options. "I'm a burger and fries guy." He closes his menu. "Easy choice."

"I think I'll try the spinach and sausage meatloaf. I love mashed potatoes." I close my menu too and drink the water that's already at the table.

"How's your throat holding up?" Jack asks.

"It's alright. I'll live." I smile before guzzling down some more water. "What are you going to do with all that prize money?" I inquire, changing the subject.

"We're hoping you'll both use that money to come to Nashville to work with us," Will interjects, joining our conversation.

"Don't need that much money for a plane ticket," Jack responds.

"No," Will says, folding his hands together on the table and leaning forward. "But it could help you guys get started. You can get a place together, and Alyssa and I can help with money at first to get you guys on your feet."

I put my hand up for him to stop. "Whoa, whoa, whoa. You want me and Jack to move away from our families and live together?"

"A lot of bands share a place when they're just starting out," Alyssa adds. "It helps keep costs down while you try to get signed with a record label."

Jack fidgets with the straw in his water, keeping his eyes fixed on the table. He sure seems uncomfortable. "I don't know," he mutters.

"You don't know if you want to live in Nashville or you don't know if you want to be in a duo with me?" I ask, feeling nervous about what his answer might be.

He raises his eyes from the table but still doesn't meet mine. "Both."

I was afraid of that. Even though we didn't see each other much all day, when we did, he seemed distant. We barely said a word on our way over to the restaurant, but I was hoping it was just because he felt awkward that he won, and I didn't. I was hoping whatever it was would blow over. That doesn't seem likely now.

"So, you don't want to sing with me." I can't look at him.

I spent the whole day warming up to the idea and just got my heart broken at Atlanta Idol. Now the only excitement left is disappearing fast. Would Will and Alyssa manage me as a solo act? I don't want to completely turn down their offer. I researched their company online earlier in the day and saw that they're managing seven other artists in country music and Christian contemporary music. All of their artists are signed to major labels and debuted high on the Billboard charts. This is an opportunity I don't want to give up.

Jack clears his throat. "I didn't exactly say that."

"Well, what exactly did you say then?" Frustration and anger bubble up inside me. If we weren't in a restaurant having a celebratory dinner surrounded by family and friends, I just might have raised my voice, despite how much it's ailing. I try my very best to keep my tone even.

Jack remains silent.

"The numbers on YouTube are undeniable," Will says, cutting in again. "There's already a demand for your music. Together."

"Don't know about that," Jack speaks up. "I won. By myself."

Alyssa raises her eyebrows. "Well, they couldn't vote for you two together, but you were both the top vote getters."

Jack lets out a long, frustrated sigh. "Look, I appreciate all this. I really do. But I just think I can do this on my own. I never pictured myself in a duo or group or nothing like that." He seems annoyed by the whole thing.

I'm more and more irritated by the second. He's being so selfish. We're being given the chance to do this together, but he'd rather pursue it on his own than be stuck with me.

"You'd be lucky to sing with my Ollie," my mama interrupts, appearing just as aggravated. She had been talking to Kat and Hanna, but she must have overheard our conversation.

Jack's parents are chatting with Brett and Ryder at the other end of the table. Clearly, they haven't gotten wind of what's going on at our end.

"But you certainly don't need to do us any favors," she continues. "Ollie can do this on her own, too."

"Mama, please," I beg, the embarrassment intensifying from my mama standing up for me.

"I don't mean to offend anyone," Jack relents. "There's a lot going on right now. I don't want to jump into this without thinking it through."

Will nods, his face relaxing, visibly relieved that the argument seems to be passing. "That's understandable. Smart man."

After we order our food and it arrives, Jack and I eat in silence. Everyone else continues to chat with each other, but we just eat. We nod at all the right times while Will and Alyssa tell us more about where their company is located in Nashville and what it's like to live in Music City. I'm glad they keep on talking because it means that Jack and I don't have to. When the waitress comes around asking if anyone wants dessert, my mama refuses and informs everyone that we're leaving.

"I have an early drive back to Summerville in the morning, and the girls need some rest. It's been a trying day." She thanks Will and Alyssa for dinner as she gets up. "Come on, y'all."

Kat, Hanna, and I rise to our feet, expressing our gratitude to Will and Alyssa, too.

"You have our card," Will says. "We'd love to meet up anywhere, anytime if you want to move forward with us. We're really interested in representing a country duo, specifically you two. Please think about it."

I peer down at Jack who refuses to look up at me. The decision-making is definitely over. Jack has closed this door for both of us. I hear him mumble goodbye as we walk away.

"You dodged a bullet, baby," my mama says, holding the door open.

"Yeah. Who needs him? He seems so self-centered. Let him try on his own," Kat adds.

My mama and Kat go ahead of me and Hanna.

"Are you okay?" Hanna asks, looping her arm through mine while we walk side by side.

I shake my head, tears forming in my eyes. "Not really. I just want to go home."

"We'll be there soon enough. Come on now. No boo-hooin'. He ain't worth it."

We continue to stroll through the charming, historic neighborhood, passing bungalow homes and boutique shops. I try to enjoy my last night in Atlanta, but I just can't. The adorable scenery is lost on me. My mind is still back in the restaurant. There are so many things I want to say to Jack. I want to talk about Will's and Alyssa's offer and see if there's a way to work it out. I have to remind myself, though, that he doesn't want to sing with me. That's the root of it all. He just doesn't want to be with me, and that's what hurts the most. How could I have been so wrong about Jack? The boy I've been hanging out with all week is not the boy in that restaurant tonight. I want to know what changed. I want to talk to him without anyone else around. Just the two of us. But we're all leaving in the morning, and I'm afraid I won't get the chance.

My mama turns around slightly. "We don't need another unreliable musician type hurting this family. I won't allow it. I just won't," she declares, expressing her distaste for Jack one more time, as if it wasn't clear enough already.

I stay quiet, letting her think my silence means I agree with her. I don't, though. Deep down in my soul, I know Jack is different. He isn't just some "unreliable musician type" or a "silly boy," as my mama and Kat call him. I can't let him go. I don't want to. I just keep on thinking of Jack and wishing we could get back to "American Honey."

Fourteen

In front of the mirror the next morning, I coat my eyelashes with mascara. The hotel room is quiet since Kat and Hanna went to Starbucks to get drinks and snacks for our drive home. My mama already left a couple hours ago to get back to the store by eight o'clock. On my tippy toes, I lean in closer to the glass to be sure to get my lashes just right. The unexpected, thunderous knocking on our room's door startles me, almost making me slip and smear a black line down my face. I figure it's probably Kat and Hanna back from their Starbucks run.

"Did y'all forget your keys?" I ask, opening the door. I gasp when I see Jack standing before me. "Oh, uh," I stammer, "I wasn't expecting you." I'm immediately embarrassed because he's getting a glimpse of me in my pink nightgown with my ratty bedhead and only one eye with mascara on.

It doesn't take long, though, for the anger from the night before to replace my humiliation. I fold my arms across my chest and wait for him to speak.

Jack shoves his hands in his pockets. "Aren't you going to invite me in?"

"No."

"Ollie." He raises his eyebrows in a hopeful and apologetic way.

I shake my head. "Why should I bother with you?" I know it sounds harsh, but I don't care. Okay, I do care, but a part of me wants his feelings to be hurt just like mine are.

He lets out an exasperated sigh. "Look, let me come in. I need to talk to you."

I pretend to think about it for a few seconds before opening the door wider to let him in. I definitely want to hear what he has to say.

We go over to the couch and sit down, not saying a word to each other. After a few minutes that seem to last an eternity, the silence and Jack's uneasiness are unbearable.

"Well, say what you need to say. I'm listening." I nod at him to go ahead.

"I'm sorry for the way everything went down last night. I didn't mean to hurt your feelings, or insult you or your family. I'm truly sorry for the way I acted." He stares directly into my eyes, proving his sincerity.

As each second passes, I soften towards him again. This is the Jack I've gotten to know all week. This is the boy who I'm becoming fast friends with. But this is also the boy who hurt me.

"Thanks for apologizing, but I think it's best if we go our separate ways." I bite my lip so I won't cry.

Jack takes my hand, clasping it to his. "You don't mean that."

"Don't you? You said you don't want to be with me. In a duo that is," I quickly clarify.

"If I didn't want to be with you, then I wouldn't be here right now." He lets go of my hand and stands up, walking back and forth in front of the couch. "Everything got messed up. It was happening so fast, and I guess I sorta freaked out. But I want to do this."

"You do?" My heart speeds up with excitement, but I'm still skeptical. "What made you change your mind?"

He smiles slightly. "Ryder and Brett. They told me what an idiot I was. They're right." He stops pacing and sits down next to me again. "I've been watching our duets online all morning. We've got something that could work."

"Could work? You still don't sound too sure."

"Well, there ain't no guarantees in this business, but I think we ought to give it a shot."

I shrug, turning away. "I don't know, Jack."

"Now you're backing out?" he asks in confusion.

"No. But I just think we both need to be one hundred percent committed to this." I study his eyes again. "And I'm not convinced that you are."

"Oh, I'm committed. Completely. I want this. I want you," Jack starts, brushing his hand against mine, "to sing with me." He grins broadly. "I want us to sing together."

I lean back, moving away from him. "I don't know," I repeat, hearing my mama's concerns echo through my head.

"Come on, Ollie."

"Are we really going to do this?" I'm thrilled and scared all at once, which seems to be a recurring feeling these days.

"Yes," Jack says, nodding. "Let's do this."

"Okay," I agree, giving him a huge smile.

Jack holds out his hand with his pinky finger raised. "Pinky swear?"

I laugh, rolling my eyes. "Jack."

He doesn't put his hand down, though. He continues to stare at me with his lips slanted in an adorable grin. "Well?"

I grab his pinky with mine when we lock eyes. That simple gesture is all it takes. We're in this together now.

After deciding that we'll tell our families first about our decision and then call Will and Alyssa, I walk Jack to the door.

"Okay," he says, stepping into the hallway. "I'll talk to you real soon." He turns to face me, leaning against the doorframe. "By the way, I like how you're rocking that nightgown. You're gonna be such a trendsetter." He grins, obviously teasing me.

I can't help but laugh. "You forgot about the bird's nest on my head."

Jack chuckles, too, and then leans in to give me a hug. "You're beautiful no matter what," he whispers in my ear.

When we pull apart, we both smile shyly at each other.

"See ya later, baby," Jack says quietly in his deep, Southern drawl, turning to walk away.

I give him a small wave, closing the door and leaning on it for support once it's shut. I can't believe what just happened. We're a duo. And he told me in the sweetest way that he thinks I'm pretty. But most importantly, we're together now, even if only professionally. I know in my heart it's the right thing for both of us. Now all I have to do is convince my mama.

Fifteen

"Are you crazy?" Kat shouts from the back of her Jeep. She's putting our bags in while Hanna and I clean out some of the leftover trash from our drive down at the beginning of the week.

"No!" I shoot back, grabbing empty cups out of the drink holders.

"I think it's a good thing. Don't be such a downer, Kat. You're always telling Ollie she's gonna be a singer. She's going after it now." Hanna is clearly on my side, but Kat's disapproval is just the beginning of what I'll have to face when I get home.

Kat climbs into the driver's seat. "I just don't think it's a good idea to rely on somebody who's so wishy-washy to help you make your dreams come true."

I get into the passenger seat while Hanna settles into the backseat. "He isn't wishy-washy. He made a mistake at first, but he's on board now," I argue.

"You can't always have it your way, Kat," Hanna points out in a sassy tone.

The three of us fall silent as we pull away from the hotel and head toward the highway. It's awfully early in the trip to already be in a tiff. At least we don't have that far to go. Jack's drive back is much longer.

I wonder if he and the boys are on the road yet. I'm tempted to text message him but decide against it. I don't want to seem too pushy or seem like I think we're best friends now just because we're a duo. We're starting a professional partnership, and I have to try my best to keep it that way. Oh, who am I fooling? I often think about what it would feel like to kiss him.

"Turn that down!" Hanna hollers from the backseat when we're about half an hour outside of Summerville. "I'm calling Ryder."

I glance at Kat who simply rolls her eyes, so I lower the volume on the Lady Antebellum album that has been blaring through the speakers.

"I saw that," Hanna says.

I turn around slightly to see her staring right at the rearview mirror where there's a clear view of Kat's eye roll.

"I don't care," Kat mumbles.

Luckily, Hanna ignores the comment.

They aren't getting along any better than when we left Atlanta. I feel like it's my fault somehow, but I'm not backing down. Hanna's support is enough to help me stand up to Kat, but nerves fire off in my stomach when I think of what my mama will say.

"Hey, sweetie," Hanna greets Ryder.

My ears perk up since I want to know where the boys are and what they're doing. Well, what Jack is doing.

Hanna chats for a little bit with Ryder about nothing much, and then I hear her say, "Yeah, of course she's here. We're still in the car." She pauses for a few seconds and then laughs. "I'll tell her. Okay, bye."

I assume that Jack has relayed a message to me through Ryder and Hanna. I'm over the moon that he's thinking of me, and I'm dying to know what he said.

"Kat, Brett says not to forget about him and all the special times you shared together this week." Hanna giggles.

"Oh, please," Kat responds with a pained expression at the mere thought of Brett. He really does seem like a good guy. What's her problem?

"And he says to call him any time."

"Right. I'll do just that." Her voice drips with sarcasm.

After listening to their exchange, I'm overcome by disappointment. Jack didn't tell Ryder to tell Hanna to tell me anything. There's no mention of Jack at all.

"What about Jack?" I blurt out without thinking. My curiosity has gotten the better of me.

"What about him?" Hanna asks, her lips curling into smirk.

"Oh, nothing. I mean... Did Ryder say anything about him?"

"Nope. Just call him if you want to talk to him. Better to be direct and go after what you want."

My cheeks go hot. "I don't want him. I was just wondering."

"Uh, huh. Sure." Hanna is acting like Miss Know-It-All and like she's so great because she's dating

Ryder. It's getting under my skin. That's for darn sure.

"Are y'all official now? How's that really going to work? He's in North Carolina."

"We're exclusive, if that's what you're asking." There's her over-confident tone again. "I've been thinking maybe I'll go to college in Carolina."

I shake my head. "I thought you were planning to go to community college near home with me."

"Well, plans change. You know all about that," Hanna replies flatly with a hint of bitterness in her voice. Maybe she isn't as enthusiastic about me moving to Nashville as she initially let on. I haven't really thought about it until now, but moving to Nashville with Jack means giving up going to college in Georgia with Hanna.

"If you want to make God laugh, tell him your plans," Kat chimes in.

"Why don't you move to Nashville with me and Jack?" I suggest to Hanna.

"And always be stuck as a third wheel following you guys around? No, thanks."

I let out a frustrated sigh. "It sounds better than moving to another state just to follow a guy you barely know."

"Why? Isn't that exactly what you're doing?" she shoots back.

I'm getting angrier and angrier by the second. I know she's sort of right, but the situation is so much different. "It isn't the same at all, and you know it. Jack and I will be working together."

"I believe that. There's no way you'd ever go for Jack. You never go for any boys because you're too scared." Hanna knows she can push my buttons when it comes to how differently we approach boys. She's being downright mean, and what's worse is that she's intending to do just that.

"Shut up, Hanna," Kat snaps at her, "or I'll let you out right here, and you can walk the rest of the way. You're miserable today."

"You're miserable every day," Hanna barks.

"Stop it!" I shout. "Just stop it. This is getting ridiculous. We're fighting like cats and dogs." I breathe a sigh of relief when they don't say anything. "I think we just need a little break from each other. It's been a long week."

"Ain't that the truth," Kat agrees.

I turn the stereo back up again, and we don't say another word to each other until we pull up to Hanna's house. With a simple "Bye, y'all," she gets out of the car, grabs her bags from the back, and heads hastily to her front door. When her mama opens it, Kat and I smile big and wave like nothing is wrong before we speed off. I pray that our argument will blow over, but I know there are some real problems we need to talk about eventually. First up, getting through the difficult conversation with my mama, then I'll deal with Hanna. Everyone keeps saying they want me to be a singer and follow my dreams, but they sure aren't making it easy to do.

"Hey, sweet pea!" my mama hollers after the door to our house swings open. She's there to greet me right when we drive up.

I jump out of the car and run straight into her arms, inhaling her sweet perfume. It's so good to be home.

"Come on, Kat," my mama shouts, waving to Kat to come inside.

I follow her into the kitchen where she has freshly baked chocolate chip cookies waiting for me. My favorite.

"Sit down. Talk to me." She pulls out a chair for me before grabbing plates and glasses from the cabinet and milk from the refrigerator. "How are you holding up?"

"Fine, I guess. It was so much fun up until that dinner," I begin. I stop myself, though. I need to tell her about Jack, and Alyssa, and Will, and the Nashville plan. I know I can tell her anything, but I'm still nervous after the way she reacted towards Jack.

She must notice my face drop. "What is it, baby?" She sits down across from me, her eyes fixed intensely on mine.

"I have to tell you something," I say, picking up a cookie to nibble on. I focus on the perfectly distributed bits of chocolate for a few long seconds before putting the cookie down and meeting my mama's eyes.

"Well, go on then."

I take a deep breath, letting it out slowly. "I talked to Jack this morning before we left."

My mama puts her hand up to stop me. "I know where this is going. Did you two make up? Are you seeing this boy now? Is that what you're telling me?"

"No," I respond, shaking my head, slightly confused as to why she would jump to that conclusion. "That's not it."

"What then?"

"He changed his mind. We decided that we want to sing together." I pause for a second, not quite able to read her expression, so I continue in a hurry before I lose my nerve. "We're going to work with Will and Alyssa. We really want to do this."

"You're telling me you want to move to Nashville with a boy you hardly know based on something two random managers outside a little singing contest told you?" Disbelief and frustration wash over her face.

My body stiffens. I probably would have gotten a better reaction if I had admitted to dating Jack. "Atlanta Idol isn't little, and Will and Alyssa aren't random. They've been so nice to us, and they manage up-and-coming *and* successful artists."

She stands up in a huff. "I don't know, Ollie. I don't know about this at all," she says, waving her arm in the air as she stomps into the living room and flops down on the couch.

I follow her and sit next to her. "I know it sounds like a long shot, but I want to give it a try. I know I can do this. Jack and I can do this. Together."

"How do you know? You just met him. You don't know anything about him. He was so against this just yesterday. Musician types never stick around. You don't know if he can commit to this."

I turn away from her. "He isn't Daddy," I disagree quietly.

"I'm just trying to protect you. That's my job. I've been down this road. Lord knows I have." She pauses briefly. "Look at me, baby."

I finally meet her big, blue eyes with mine. "I want to do this, Mama. *Please*."

"You don't have to, you know. We talked about college. You and Hanna had a plan."

"No, you talked about college more than Hanna and I ever did. And I still might go at some point. But for now, this is the path I want to follow."

My mama sighs loudly. "I know music is in your blood. I know you're a performer. I can't take that away from you, and I certainly wouldn't try." She grabs my hand and squeezes it gently. "I'm sorry I'm so selfish sometimes."

"What do you mean?"

"I'm scared. You're leaving me for music. This isn't the first time this is happening to me." She bites her lip, her eyes filling with tears.

I move closer to her and put my arm around her. "I'm never leaving you, Mama. This isn't like when Daddy disappeared. Not at all."

"Yes, it is. But if you're sure you really want to do this…"

"Don't make me choose. Pursuing music is not choosing Daddy over you. I know that's what you're thinking."

She glances down and nods. "Guilty."

"We'll always be with each other no matter where life takes us." My eyes water too, but I manage a small laugh. "You're stuck with me." I embrace her and hold her tightly for a long time.

"Thanks, baby," she says when we finally pull apart. "I love you."

"I love you, too."

My mama gives me a warm smile. "I'd like to get to know Jack better."

"Okay."

"How about now?" She's always ready for the next adventure, even when it makes her nervous.

"He lives in North Carolina. I told you that," I remind her, dismissing her suggestion.

"The truck's out front." She grabs her keys from the coffee table and tosses them to me. "You drive."

Sixteen

By five o'clock on Tuesday morning, my mama's truck is all packed up, and we're ready to make the drive to Chapel Hill. I wanted a couple days to relax at home before we make the journey to Jack's house. Besides, I had to make sure it was okay with him and his parents. Luckily, they're on board. I don't really know how I feel about going to Jack's hometown. Part of me is excited to see where he's from and where he grew up. But the other part of me is really nervous to see how our families will get along, aside from dinner in Atlanta. It's real important for my mama to like them and declare that they are "good people" for her to warm up to the move to Nashville.

My mama, Kat, and I take turns driving just over eight hours to Chapel Hill. Needless to say, we're exhausted from the long trip. It would have been so much easier to fly, but my mama doesn't have money in her budget to buy three plane tickets. As we drive through Jack's neighborhood, I can't help but notice that the houses are much nicer than where we live. I'm used to houses that are small and spread out, but this is an actual neighborhood. I see a community clubhouse, tennis courts, and walking trails among the rows and rows of trees. Our house is a one story, brick, ranch style house that looks more like a tiny schoolhouse from the seventies on the outside than a home. As we get closer and closer to Jack's house, I have a feeling his will be much different.

"That's it," Kat announces, pointing to Jack's house after she reads the directions I had scribbled down.

"Yeah. Stop here, Mama," I instruct her, gazing out the window. Just as I suspected, his house is gorgeous. It's picture perfect, like it belongs on a postcard or in a magazine.

I walk up to the front door ahead of my family. Before I have a chance to ring the bell, the door swings open.

"Come on in, y'all! Welcome to Chapel Hill!" Jack's mom is bursting with enthusiasm. "How was the drive?"

"Good but long," I admit, stepping inside.

"Well, you're here now, and y'all can relax." She smiles sweetly, reaching for the sweatshirt I'm holding in my hands. "I'll hang this up for you." She's putting it in a small closet just off the foyer when I hear my mama and Kat walk through the doorway.

"Welcome!" Jack's mom greets them with a warm grin. "Nice to see you again," she says, extending her hand to shake theirs.

My mama smiles politely. "Thank you. Lovely to see you, too." She glances around the room, her eyes practically bugging out at the striking archways, classy furniture, and hardwood floors. The decorative detail is certainly stunning, like on one of those interior design TV shows. "You have such a gorgeous home."

Kat nods in agreement. "It's darling."

"Thank you. I'm glad you could visit. I was tickled pink when Jack said y'all were driving all this way just to spend time with us!" She leans forward to put her hand on my mama's arm. "If our kids are going to be working together, it's best to get to know each other now."

"Well, I'd like all of us to dine together later. Right now, we have to find a hotel. We just wanted to say hello first and see if you have any recommendations on where to stay." My mama looks down with a sheepish grin, clearly embarrassed. "This trip was sort of on a whim. I didn't plan out all the details."

"Don't worry about it. Y'all can stay with us." Jack's mom nods her head with certainty.

Panic rises up in my throat. Stay with Jack's family? In his house? With my family here, too? This is way too much right off the bat. I don't want such close quarters to ruin the chances of my mama liking these people. But I also don't want Jack's mom to think we're rude not to stay in her house.

"Here?" I mumble, my mind in full on worry mode. "Miss Sara, that's so kind of you," I say slowly, trying to find the right words, "but we don't want to cause any inconvenience."

"None whatsoever! We'd love to have y'all here." Her smile is so sincere and inviting that it's even harder to tell her no. "We only have one guestroom, so I was thinking that Jolene and Kat can stay in there, and Ollie, you can stay in Jack's room."

In Jack's room? I feel like I'm in a sauna. It's scorching hot like one of the worst summer days in Georgia. I know my face must be scarlet. "With Jack?" I croak out, my voice sounding embarrassingly shrill.

His mom lets out a loud laugh that echoes through the living room. "Don't be ridiculous. He'll stay in our bonus room on the couch."

I'm even more humiliated because she laughed, even though it doesn't seem like she's purposely trying to be hurtful. I glance at Kat who's smirking too, but my mama still has her polite smile plastered across her face. She seems as uncomfortable as I am, but she's hiding it a tad better than me.

"Speaking of Jack, where is he anyway?" I ask, trying to shift the focus of the conversation.

"He went with his dad to pick up a few things for me from the store. They should be back any minute." She pauses for a second. "If y'all want to go get your bags, I'll show you to your rooms."

"I don't know about this. I feel like we're imposing. A hotel recommendation is fine, really," my mama says, reiterating my sentiments.

Sara shakes her head. "Nonsense. Y'all are staying with us. Now, go on and get your luggage."

We reluctantly head out to the car. When we return, Sara brings me to Jack's room and then takes my mama and Kat to the guestroom. As soon as I enter my singing partner's room, I notice all the baseball memorabilia. Posters on the walls, baseballs and bobble heads on his dresser and nightstand. Everything is baseball, except for a framed portrait of Elvis next to his flat screen TV and a guitar in the corner of the room. I survey his space, making a mental note of every detail. I put my bags on his bed and go over to the wall to study the posters and pictures. There are a lot of photos of Jack and his teammates playing baseball alongside posters of professional athletes. I giggle when I see a small poster of Carrie Underwood.

"You moving in?"

I jump back, startled by that deep voice that I've come to know so well. I whirl around to see Jack leaning on the doorframe with a playful grin directed at me. "Uh…" I mumble, rushing over to his bed to grab my leopard print luggage. "No. I just…well, I…" What the heck is wrong with me? "Your mom told me to come in here," I tell him, finally completing a sentence.

"In town for five minutes," he says, looking at his cell phone, even though the screen isn't lit up, "and you've already kicked me out of my own room."

"Sorry. We told your mom we'd go to a hotel. She wouldn't hear of it, though. Look, I can stay in the bonus room. No big deal. You can have your room back."

Jack chuckles, shaking his head. "I'm just yanking your chain. It's fine. I'm glad you're here."

"In Chapel Hill or in your room?" I blurt out before thinking about what I'm really asking.

He rolls his eyes and laughs again. "Why don't we get something to eat? You hungry?"

"Sure. Yeah. Good idea. Let's go." I really need to relax and get a grip.

Since it's around four o'clock, we decide to just grab some drinks at a nearby café. We take Jack's truck and Kat tags along. To her surprise, Brett is waiting in the parking lot when we pull in. Jack had texted him that we would be here. I think it's pretty funny, but Kat doesn't seem amused. She had to know she might see him, though. We're in Chapel Hill, and he lives here. Come on now.

"There's my little Kitty Kat," Brett says to Kat when we get out of the car.

I don't think she was expecting his new nickname for her because she actually smiles an honest to goodness, genuine smile at him, instead of her usual sneer. Or maybe she *was* expecting it. Have they been in touch? I can't imagine why.

"Hey," she replies simply, trying to conceal the grin that's spreading across her face.

What in the world is going on? Jack and I exchange confused glances as we all approach the door of the café.

Brett grins, opening it for me. "What's the word, Ollie?"

"Weird," I respond, going inside.

Things are getting stranger and stranger by the minute. First, I'm coerced into staying in Jack's bedroom, and now Brett and Kat are getting along. What next? Pigs soaring through the sky?

After getting our drinks, we decide to go to the lake near Jack's house. Jack brings his guitar, and we sit by the shore in the grass, just hanging out. Brett and Kat are a few feet away from us engrossed in a game of 'Would You Rather.' Count that as another odd thing to happen today. Jack plays his guitar, strumming another song I don't recognize.

"A Jack Bradley original?" I ask, leaning back with my legs outstretched. I love feeling the blades of grass between my fingers.

"Yes, ma'am. Just a little something I started working on last week."

"Does it have lyrics?"

"Nope, not yet." Jack continues to play a beautiful melody.

I close my eyes, and without even thinking, I start singing. The words flow as easily from my mouth as the music flows from Jack's fingertips.

"That's good. We should write that down," he says, putting his guitar down in his lap.

I nod. "Keep playing."

"Nah, let's pick it up later when we can get those words on paper."

I reluctantly agree, standing up when Jack does. "Where are you going?"

"Take a walk with me." He smiles, staring into my eyes briefly before directing his attention to Brett and Kat. "Come on, y'all."

Jack and I stroll ahead of Brett and Kat on the walking trails around the lake. For two people who didn't like each other last week, they're certainly chummy now. Well, Brett has always had a fondness for Kat. Whatever. I can't think about them right now. I'm too worried about how my mama and Jack's parents are getting along. They've been together back at the house all this time. This is make it or break it time in terms of Nashville. But then again, I don't have to listen to my mama all the time anymore. I wonder if I can actually go against her wishes, though. I don't want to wind up as one of those people who never speaks to their own mama ever again. That's not an option for me. I already lost my daddy.

"Cat got your tongue?"

I shift back to reality, realizing that Jack is talking to me. "Huh?"

"You're unusually quiet."

"I have a lot on my mind."

"Sharing is caring," Jack says with that teasing grin.

I roll my eyes and sigh. "I'm just worried that our parents won't get along, and then I can't go to Nashville with you."

"Whoa. What do you mean?" he wonders, putting his hand up in surprise.

"Just that if my mama doesn't like what's going on, then I can't go. I need her approval."

"No, you don't. You're a big girl, Ollie."

"I knew I shouldn't have worn these shorts," I confess, tugging at the sides of my tiny denim cutoffs. "Other kids have teased me since I was younger that I have thunder thighs."

Jack frowns. "That's ridiculous. People are idiots. But anyway, that's not what I said. I didn't literally mean you're big. Stay with me here." He takes a deep breath. "You're like a bullet train barreling off the track."

"I'm just saying—" I start, but he cuts me off.

"Listen, I know you want to make your family happy, and you want to keep the peace, but you have to do what you want to do. It's your life."

"I know. I wish it was that simple."

"If you let your mom control your life, and you give up this opportunity, you're going to wind up resenting her. Guaranteed." He bows his head, giving me a knowing look. "But let's not jump to conclusions. My parents are great people. I'm sure everyone is getting on just fine."

"I hope so," I say, sighing.

Jack's cell phone goes off in his pocket. "Can you hold this for a second?" he asks, handing me his drink from the café, his guitar in his other hand. He reaches into his pants pocket and yanks out his phone. "Hey, Mom. What's up?"

I don't get any information from his side of the conversation since he keeps saying, "okay" and "yeah." But right before he hangs up, he says we'll be there soon.

"Where?" I inquire while he puts the phone away then takes his drink back.

"They're just about ready to head out for dinner. We're going to one of my favorite restaurants." He smiles, putting his hand over his stomach. "Mm. It's so good."

"Should we head back then?"

Jack nods and turns around. "We're going for Mexican food."

"Okay. I'm down," Brett responds. "It's going to blow your mind," he continues, turning to Kat, to which he gets her usual eye roll but also a tiny smile.

Seventeen

We all make our way back to Jack's house to meet up with our parents. Jack tells me the restaurant is in Durham, so we have a twenty-minute drive. He assures me it's worth every minute, though. I don't really mind because I like seeing new places and getting to experience the things that Jack loves.

When we all arrive at the restaurant, we settle in at two of the burgundy leather booths. I sit at one with Kat, Jack, and Brett and our parents sit at the other. It's the natural divide, the kids' table and the grown-ups' table. We fill up on burritos, enchiladas, and tacos. Jack and Brett are right. It's all delicious.

"We have to get some fried ice cream," Jack announces after our dinner dishes are cleared.

"Oh, no," Kat groans. "I'm stuffed. I couldn't eat another thing."

"I'm pretty full, too," I agree.

Brett moves his head disapprovingly. "Typical girls. You gotta learn to pack it away like us guys."

"Why?" Kat asks, glaring at him in disbelief. "We're not guys."

"I don't know," he mutters, turning away.

That concludes more of the pointless back-and-forth they've been engaging in for hours. At least they're pretty much getting along, even if their conversations don't exactly go anywhere.

Jack goes ahead and orders the fried ice cream anyway. Kat and I have a taste, and it's amazing.

"Wow," I admit, taking a little bit more from Jack's dish. "I've never had this before, but I love it."

He smiles, raising his eyebrows at me. "Imagine that. Trying new things with me and they ain't so bad. Get used to it."

Heat rushes to my cheeks, but I'm not sure why. I know he's talking about our new career together, but what he said makes me nervous in a different kind of way. I shrug it off and change the subject.

"Looks like you were right about them," I concede, pointing to our parents at the next table. They're laughing and appear to be enjoying each other's company. My mama isn't smiling her fake smile or doing her polite laugh either. Her face is relaxed, and her reactions are genuine.

"I'm always right."

"Yeah. Yeah. Sure."

Jack whips out his phone. "I'm going to call Will and Alyssa."

"Why?" I ask, staring at him curiously.

"It looks like Nashville's a go. Better to let them know sooner than later."

I breathe deeply. "Wait. Don't do it yet. Let's at least talk to my mama and your parents after dinner. Then, we can call."

Jack agrees, so we wait until we get back to his house to sit down with our parents and see what they're thinking.

"I'm warming up to it," my mama says, taking a seat next to me in Jack's living room.

"I just worry about the living situation," Jack's dad, Ty, adds. "I want to be able to trust you two."

"Have I ever given you a reason not to trust me?" Jack counters, obviously annoyed by the insinuation. "Besides, Ollie and I are adults."

"Age doesn't make you an adult," Ty continues. "Maturity does. I want to be sure that you can both handle all this."

"I don't want to be a grandmother yet," my mama chimes in.

I want to crawl in a hole and hide. This conversation just took a turn for the worse. I'm so embarrassed that I can't look anyone in the eye. I desperately want it to be over.

"I hear that," Sara concurs.

Jack jumps to his feet in a huff. "I don't know what y'all are talking about. Ollie and I aren't starting a family. We're starting a career. We aren't even dating!"

"Mistakes happen." Ty shrugs, taking a sip of his coffee.

"This is the most ridiculous thing I've ever heard. Y'all are acting like we're animals at the zoo. If we're caged up together, then it's bound to happen." His face is a deep shade of pink from anger and possibly embarrassment, but mostly anger. "I'll have you know that if Ollie and I want to have sex, we'll do it. It won't matter if we're living together or not."

Okay, now I want to crawl in a hole and die. I can't believe what I'm hearing. I'm so far beyond mortified that I can't even think of a word to express how I feel. The calm, cool, collected boy I met in Atlanta has a fiery side that I haven't seen before. He isn't afraid to speak his mind, which reminds me of myself in most situations, except this one. As awkward as this is, Jack does have a point. And he's even hotter when he gets all riled up like that.

"That's enough, son." Ty's stern face shows signs of annoyance, too. "Sit down." He takes a long breath before speaking and leans forward, putting his elbows on his knees. "Look, we're your parents, so we want to protect you. But we also don't want to stand in the way of your dreams."

"I just want to say something." I finally find my voice again. "I'm not going into this with the intention of doing anything other than singing with Jack. I won't lose my focus because this is my dream," I glance Jack's way, "*our* dream, and I won't let anything mess it up. I know better. Jack does, too."

My mama wraps her arm around me. "That's right. My baby has a good head on her shoulders." She pauses, looking down. "As long as I'm kept in the loop and involved in what's going on, y'all have my blessing."

"Thanks, Mama," I say in surprise, hugging her. I turn my head to Jack whose face has returned to its normal color. We give each other a hopeful look, but stifle our smiles. We still don't know what his parents will say.

"We agree with Jolene," Sara reveals at last.

"So, you're okay with this?" Jack asks to make sure.

His parents hesitate, exchanging an anxious glance.

"As okay with it as we'll ever be, I suppose. We support you. Both of you," Ty confirms.

Jack and I breathe sighs of relief. It's really real now. We have the support of our parents, and that's what I wanted most.

After hugging them and thanking them and telling them we won't let them down, Jack walks me back to his room.

He sits down on edge of the bed and gets out his phone again. "I'm calling Will and Alyssa now. This is it, okay?"

I nod, staying quiet so I won't protest any more. I know it's time to move forward, despite the doubts that still linger in the silence.

A few seconds later, Jack greets Will and engages in some small talk at first, but it isn't long before he shares our big news. "The reason I'm calling is to tell you that Ollie and I are on board. We're coming to Nashville."

Eighteen

Jack and I are going to meet up with Will and Alyssa in Nashville in a week. In the meantime, they're going to try to find a place for us to live and keep in touch with their progress. We'll probably stay in a hotel at first, but they told us to pack as if we're moving because we'll be there a long time before getting to go home again. They're going to get right to work on getting us studio time and songs to record so that we can do a showcase for record executives in the near future. It's all unfolding at a rapid speed, just like the contest in Atlanta. I'm slowly getting used to the fast pace and how quickly things can change, but it'll still take more time for it all to sink in.

I put my pajamas on and sit down on Jack's bed. Am I really going to sleep in his bed? It seems so weird. I don't get under the covers, but lay down on top of his comforter instead. Ironically, I'm anything but comfortable. I sit back up and reach for my cell phone on his nightstand. Hanna and I have only communicated through text messages since the feud in the car on the way back to Summerville, but I need to talk to someone. I don't want to bother Kat, especially with my mama in the same room, and I have to make amends with Hanna, not just by text. Besides, I miss hearing her voice. When we aren't arguing, she always makes me feel better.

"Hey, Hanny," I say when she answers her phone. I hope using my childhood nickname for her will help somehow.

"Hey, Olliepop," she replies in her familiar sweet tone.

I breathe a sigh of relief when I hear my nickname, too. Now I know she isn't that mad anymore. "We're okay, right?"

"I told you in my text that I was sorry. I just needed some time to adjust to your new life, and it came out rude."

"Okay. I wanted to make sure. I'm sorry, too. I know all of this is new and different for everyone."

"Uh huh," she agrees. "So, what's going on? Where are you?"

I let out a hushed giggle so no one else will hear me on the phone. "In Jack's bed."

"Ollie!" She laughs, too, but much louder than me. "No, really. Where are you?"

"I'm serious. I'm in his bed. Well, technically I'm on top of it." Silence. I assume she's still trying to figure out if I'm kidding or not. "Don't get all crazy, though. He isn't here."

"Well, shut my mouth. Okay, rewind. Start from the beginning. How on Earth did you end up there of all places?"

I explain how we got stuck staying at Jack's house and how our parents accepted that we're going to move to Nashville. Then, I wait anxiously for Hanna's response.

She sighs. "So, you're really going? You're really moving away."

The finality of it breaks my heart. I hear the sadness in her voice and immediately feel sad, too. Why is this so hard? Nashville really isn't that far. But it isn't the distance. It's the separation. Hanna and I have been side by side since we were little. I see her every single day unless we're on vacation with our families, and even then, sometimes she tags along on my trip, and I do the same on hers. She's like a sister to me, more so than Kat at times.

"You can come visit, and I'll get back to Summerville when I can. My life's changing, but I'm not. I'll always be the same Ollie. I'll always be your best friend," I say, trying to reassure her the best I can.

"Are you wearing your bracelet?" Hanna asks, referring to the friendship bracelets we made for each other in fifth grade.

"Of course. You?"

"Absolutely. We're with each other no matter what then." She pauses for a second. "Ollie, I really am happy for you. I don't ever want to make you feel like I'm not. As much as I'm excited for your new adventure, I'm sort of blue, too, if that makes any sense."

I nod my head even though she can't see. "It sure does."

"I can't believe your mama is going for this," she says, chuckling a little bit. "Especially after Jack's little outburst about y'all getting it on."

I had texted her all about that particular incident. As I twirl my hair around my index finger, I can't help but laugh, too, just thinking of it. "My mama has been surprisingly cool, but I have to admit I was sure surprised by what he said."

"Would you?"

"Would I what?"

"Would you do it with Jack?"

"Do what?"

"Don't play dumb, Ollie."

I let out an exasperated sigh. "I am certainly not discussing this while I'm on his bed."

Hanna giggles mischievously. "Okay, let's take a different approach. Do you wish he was there with you right now?"

"I don't know!" I blurt out a little too loudly. I take a deep breath, hoping I can explain this to her so that she'll understand enough to drop it from now on. Talking about Jack like this makes my palms sweaty and my heart race. "I mean, he is kind of cute, but I don't want things to get weird between us. I have to live with him."

"Let me get this straight. You like him, but you just want to be friends?" she asks, sounding confused.

"It's really too soon to know if I like him, but yes, I do want to just be friends."

"Okay. Okay. I'll back off." The line goes quiet for a few seconds. "He has very kissable lips, though."

My mind wanders to Jack's adorably perfect lips, and smile, and face, and hair. Oh, is he ever attractive! I'm in a dreamlike state, thinking of how very much I do, in fact, want to smooch him. I haven't totally let my mind go there since we were in Atlanta. "Yes, he does," I whisper, unaware if I said it out loud.

"A-ha!" Hanna shouts. "What do I always say?"

Darn it. She got me.

"If you imagine kissing a certain boy, then you like him," I repeat in my best imitation of Hanna.

She cackles triumphantly. "The same goes for other things, too, you know."

"Okay, I'm hanging up now."

"Sleep well," she says, still laughing. "Oh, would you look at that! It's past midnight. Happy birthday, sweetie! Call me tomorrow."

"Thanks! I will. Love you."

"Love you, too."

I click off my phone and set it down beside me. There's no way I'll be able to "sleep well." Not here. And definitely not after that conversation. I spot Jack's guitar in the corner and decide that I need some more practice and some fresh air.

Nineteen

On Jack's back porch, I settle into one of the rocking chairs and begin to play. It sounds weird, and I can't figure out why until I realize that it probably isn't tuned right. I've watched Jack tune his guitar before, but I don't really know how. I continue to strum along, hoping something melodious will somehow develop.

"What kind of animal is dying out here?"

I abruptly stop playing and turn around to see Jack standing in the doorway wearing flannel pajama pants, a white T-shirt, and flip flops on his feet. "Very funny," I retort. "I'm practicing."

"You'll need a heck of a lot more practice if it keeps on sounding like that." He gives me a small grin, taking a seat in the rocking chair next to mine.

It isn't cold, but I have chill bumps. "Did I wake you?"

"Nah. I always sit out here past midnight." He flashes another smile my way before reaching for his guitar. "Hand it over."

"You aren't going to help me?" I wonder, using my best puppy dog face.

"I will. Just hold your horses. I want to play something first."

Before I know it, Jack is playing and singing the happy birthday song to me in his low, smooth, classic country tone. It's the first time I've heard that song with such a beautiful twang to it. I can't help but laugh out of surprise. "You remembered."

"Well, you've only mentioned it a couple dozen times and then some."

"I most certainly have not." I deny it, even though I know I've mentioned it more than once.

We glance at each other for a second, little smiles dancing across both our faces, before turning our attention to the moonlit silhouettes of the giant trees that fill Jack's backyard.

"What do you think it'll be like?" I ask, breaking the silence.

"Being nineteen? It's fun, I guess. I don't feel any different," Jack responds, running his fingers over the tiny amount of stubble that covers his chin.

"No, not that. Nashville." My voice is barely above a whisper. I'm afraid that if I say Nashville any louder, then it'll be real. It *is* real. I can shout it from the rooftops if I want to and it won't change a thing. But instead, I search Jack's face for some sort of answer that I know he doesn't have.

He looks directly into my eyes with a warm, endearing smile. "Whatever it is, we'll make the best of it, and we'll get through it together. It'll be just fine. Trust me."

I grin, too, holding his gaze. He didn't say much, but I cast my worries aside, anyway. We're a team.

It's something I can't really explain or make sense of, but I can feel it.

"You're the best," I compliment him, shoving his shoulder playfully.

Jack's lips curl into a shy, boyish grin. "I don't know about that." Before long, his face grows serious. "I'm glad we're doing this together. Really." He picks up his guitar again. "I can't wait to get to Nashville."

"I know I've been carrying on about how scared I am, but I'm actually really excited, too. This is so crazy! Obviously, I've never done anything like this in my whole life. Well, I know I'm not that old, but still. I've wanted to sing professionally and make an album since I was about three years old, if that's even possible. It's been a long time coming. That's for darn sure. Do you think we'll get signed? Oh my gosh, I've been praying that we get a record deal. Have you?"

"Yes, ma'am," Jack answers with wide eyes and his signature smile. "I've talked to Him about it a few times."

It's then that I realize I've been rambling again. I don't care, though. I'm finally allowing myself to show enthusiasm for what the future might hold for us. "If we could go on tour with anyone, who would you want it to be?"

He rolls his eyes, laughing and shaking his head. "Ain't we getting a little ahead of ourselves?"

"Come on," I urge, pushing his knee. "Dream out loud. No harm in that. Who would you pick?"

"Uh," Jack starts, hesitation in his voice. "I don't know. Maybe Carrie Underwood."

"Oh, right. The poster in your room."

His face turns crimson in a flash, and he looks away. "You saw that?" he mumbles.

"Sure did. It's cute. You have a crush on Carrie. Who doesn't? She's beautiful and talented and so sweet. I want to be just like her."

"You're already all those things."

It's my turn to blush. "Uh, thanks."

"How 'bout you? Who do you want to tour with?"

Our eyes meet again, and I rack my brain for an answer. I hope that someday Jack and I will headline our own tour, but I don't want to jinx us, so I keep that to myself. "I saw a Lady Antebellum show last year. They're awesome. I choose them."

Jack nods his approval. "Good choice." He seems like he wants to say something else, but he's holding his tongue.

"What?" I ask curiously as he stares at me with a funny expression.

"Nothing."

"Tell me."

"Nothing." He shifts around in his chair uncomfortably. "Just that I hope we have our own tour someday."

"Unbelievable," I whisper, my mouth hanging open.

"What? Does that make me sound cocky or something?"

"Not at all. I was thinking the exact same thing."

We smile at each other. There's that inexplicable connection again. We're on the same wavelength when it comes to our dreams and goals.

I sigh, slumping down in my chair. "I have no idea how we'll get to that point, but it would be amazing."

"Mmhmm," Jack agrees. "Hey, why don't we work on that song we started at the lake?"

"Great idea."

A couple minutes later, I return to the back porch with my laptop so I can type the lyrics and jot down the chords while Jack plays his guitar. We work on the song past three in the morning. We're on a roll, adding and deleting as we go along until we get it just right. It's pouring out of us so fast, which fuels our ideas even more. I knew writing with Jack would be magical. I just knew it.

"Three twenty seven," I announce, throwing my body back against the chair, the laptop still brightly lit in front of me resting on my knees. I'm exhausted yet exhilarated.

"What's that?" Jack wonders.

"The exact time we finished writing our first song together."

I Know You
Written by Jack Bradley and Ollie McKenna

Sitting on the back porch
Talking about life and dreams
Singing to each other
Trying to find our way through the melodies

When I wonder where I'm going
I find direction in you
In your laugh and in your smile
In the sparkle in your eyes
Oh, I know just where I'm going
Because I know you

Counting on you for anything
Getting along or figuring it out
Nothing we can't solve when we sing
Taking this journey song by song
Day by day

When I wonder where I'm going
I find direction in you
In your laugh and in your smile
In the sparkle in your eyes
Oh, I know just where I'm going
Because I know you

Some days it's hard
Sometimes it's easy
But even when it takes a lot

We never give up on us
No, never give up on us

When I wonder where I'm going
I find direction in you
In your laugh and in your smile
In the sparkle in your eyes
Oh, I know just where I'm going
Because I know you
Yeah, I know you

.

Twenty

"Time to greet the day, sunshine," Jack hollers from the hallway, knocking loudly on the door.

Groggily, I open my eyes and sit up for a quick second before flopping back down onto the bed.

He raps on the door a few more times. "I'm coming in. On the count of three... One, two, three."

"Hey," I mumble, face down in the pillow. There's a siren going off in my head, screaming at me to get up and get dressed because this is super embarrassing, having Jack see me with bedhead from *his* bed and zero makeup on. But most of me is too tired to care. That must be a sign that we're just friends and nothing more.

"Gotta get my clothes," Jack informs me as he begins rummaging through his dresser drawers.

I rub my eyes and pop up again, grabbing my rubber band from the nightstand to put my hair into a ponytail.

"My mom is making breakfast, if you want some. Be ready in twenty minutes." He tosses one of his baseball caps to me.

"What's this for?"

"We're heading out to the field. I've got plenty of fun planned for you, birthday girl."

"I don't think our ideas of fun are the same in this situation. I was thinking of going shopping and just relaxing for the day," I admit, trying to gently tell him no to a day of sports. "Don't get me wrong. I used to play softball when I was a kid, and I was a cheerleader for a year in high school, which *is* a sport, by the way. But I'm not feeling it today."

Jack reaches for the door with his free hand, his other one clutching his clothes. He turns back to look at me. "This is your last day in town, and then the next time I'll see you will be in Nashville. Let me show you Chapel Hill. *My* Chapel Hill. Think of it as a gift from me to you."

It's real hard to stand my ground when I stare into those sky blue, hopeful eyes. Besides, a day with Jack does sound like a great way to spend my birthday, regardless of the activity. "Okay. I'm in. But we might have to pass by the mall, too. It's only fair."

He shakes his head and chuckles. "Deal."

Jack and I arrive at his high school's baseball field about an hour later. I took longer to get ready than he wanted but tough luck. My mama always tells me that if you keep a man waiting and he's still there when you're finally ready, then he's really yours. I don't know if it exactly applies to this situation, but just for the day, Jack is all mine.

"Toss me the ball," he yells from the pitcher's mound.

I throw it to him underhanded without a lot of force, so it winds up landing way before him and rolling to his feet. "Oops," I say, shrugging my shoulders.

"I would say that you throw like a girl, but that was worse. I don't know what that was."

I sigh dramatically. "Just pitch, okay?"

"Yes, ma'am. But I have to warn you. It's been a few months, so I have to see if there's anything left in the ol' cannon."

"Blah, blah, blah," I sing, holding the bat up in my best hitter's stance.

I barely blink, and the ball is hurling towards me at incredible speed. Jack has some arm! I duck slightly and swing, but it's mostly a reflex to avoid being hit in the head by the ball. Needless to say, I miss it.

"Let me show you how to swing that thing." Jack leaves the mound and approaches me.

"Really?" I ask sarcastically. "I don't need your help. I was just surprised by your fast ball. That's all."

He disregards what I said and puts his arms around me, positioning my hand on the bat just so. "Here. Like this."

My pulse speeds up from his touch, but I try to play it cool. "This is right out of a bad movie or something." I laugh it off, but he's so close to me that I feel uncomfortable and yet right at home. Since I met Jack, I've been experiencing so many emotions that I didn't even think were possible.

I end up hitting the ball several times, and then we switch places. I'm not that great of a pitcher, but it's still fun, anyway, especially because I'm seeing a new side of Jack. He's so in his element, having fun, smiling and laughing the whole time. Jack isn't one to have a bubbly, over-the-top attitude. That's typically me, but today, it's like we traded personalities. When I round the bases, he runs to get the ball but stops to put his arms around me and steer me away from the base. He's so much more playful and touchy feely than ever before. I had no idea baseball has this effect on him, but it makes me wish we could stay on this field forever.

"Let's get cleaned up. We have a big night ahead," Jack says, winking at me as we leave his high school.

"Where are we going?" I inquire, intrigued. My birthday is shaping up to be much better than I expected.

"To my house."

"No, not right now. Later," I clarify as if I really needed to, nudging his shoulder.

"For me to know and you to find out." Jack smiles and then walks ahead of me.

I sigh and go faster to catch up to him. "You're like ten years old."

"Eleven."

I can't help but burst out laughing. "You're something else."

We get in Jack's truck and stop for some lunch before heading back to his house. He still won't tell me where he's taking me later, but he does say to wear something "chill," whatever that means. I don't have a lot of choices because I didn't pack that much.

But luckily, having a mama who's so into clothes and style helps at a time like this. She brought extra outfits for me and Kat. She always does that when we travel. She likes to have options. I know I can count on her.

In the guestroom, I browse through my mama's luggage alone since she isn't here. Neither is Kat. I texted them and found out that they went shopping. I'm a little bummed since Jack and I didn't end up stopping at the mall like I had suggested, but I remind myself that it's okay because he has a surprise for me that's sure to be amazing. After rummaging around, I finally settle on pink, flower-patterned, palazzo pants with a creamy tan, tie-front, button-up crop top. I finish my look off with sandstone platform booties and a honeycomb pendant necklace. Now I'm ready for whatever the night throws my way.

Jack, Kat, Brett, Ryder, and I arrive at an all-ages, live music club in Carrboro, the town next to Chapel Hill, a few hours later. It's small, dark, and packed with people. It has the type of atmosphere that's expected of this kind of club. I'm not surprised but not impressed either. When we pulled up, Jack assured me that this is a world famous venue and that I'd love it. I'm trying to be open-minded but not entirely convinced yet.

"Y'all want something to drink?" Brett yells over the music of Fountains of Wayne, the band performing for the night that I haven't heard of before.

We all agree, and the boys set off to the bar. Kat and I remain in silence, taking in the scene, and people watching.

"You and Jack should be on that stage," Kat shouts, breaking into my thoughts.

I laugh, shrugging my shoulders. "I don't know about that."

"You've sung together in a place bigger than this."

"We've also sung in parking lots." I sigh, but of course, no one can hear me over the music and all the club noise. "We don't even have any songs yet."

Kat fishes through her purse, clearly on a mission. "Found it!" she declares, holding up her berry blast lip gloss. "I heard some great music drifting up from the porch last night. Or was I just dreaming that?" She smiles knowingly like she's in on a secret.

I bite my bottom lip to try to suppress the smile that's forming on my lips. "Okay. Yes, we wrote our first song together."

"That's amazing!"

"I don't know if Will and Alyssa are going to like it, or if it will ever get recorded, or anything."

"You have to start somewhere. Don't sell yourself short. Writing a song is an incredible accomplishment."

It feels good to have Kat on my side, encouraging Jack and I as a duo. God love her. The support from my family and Hanna isn't always consistent, but it's there, nevertheless.

The boys rejoin us with Cokes for everyone. Brett pulls Kat aside, and they move to a corner of the club where I can see them whispering into each other's ears and laughing. They are enjoying themselves much more than I ever thought possible.

"Having a good time?" Jack asks into my ear. He stands by my side, Coke in hand, watching the band. Ryder is on the other side of Jack, bobbing his head along to the beat.

"The night's just starting," I respond, giving him an encouraging smile. I want him to feel good about taking me here, even though it isn't really my kind of music or my kind of scene, and I feel like I'm dressed wrong, too. As I glance around at the sea of jeans, t-shirts, and Converse sneakers, I know my outfit is anything but "chill." Even Jack is wearing jeans, a simple black t-shirt and flip flop sandals.

The band welcomes the crowd before launching into their next song called "The Summer Place."

"They're actually not bad," I admit to Jack.

He grins, looking pleased that I'm finally enjoying myself. If I can't beat 'em, I should just join 'em, so I nod my head along to the music like Ryder.

When the song ends, I tell them that I'm paying a visit to the little girls' room. On the way, I throw my empty Coke bottle in the recycle bin, but some of the drips get my fingers sticky. In the bathroom, I decide to wash my hands first. While I'm standing at the sink, a girl comes in who looks about my age. She has long, blonde hair, and her skin is super tan. I avert my eyes and shut the sink off.

"Hey," she greets me, "I'd know you anywhere." She's wagging her index finger back and forth at me.

I glance at her curiously, obviously startled. Am I having my first fan encounter? Maybe she saw the videos on YouTube, or she was in the audience at Atlanta Idol. It's kind of strange, but really exciting, too.

"You're Ollie McKenna," she continues with a confident nod, her hair swaying back and forth.

I nod in return, wondering what to say next. "Do I know you?" I stare into her narrow, thickly lined, hazel eyes, waiting for her to reveal how much she loves my voice.

"Well, now you do, silly. I'm Erica." She extends her hand, so I grasp it with mine.

"Nice to meet you." I'm sort of uncomfortable just standing in the bathroom chatting with a fan. It's a weird place to meet and definitely not where I want to give my first autograph. I'm about to ask if she wants to go back into the club and hang out for a while, but she speaks up instead.

"I've seen all your videos on YouTube. I followed Atlanta Idol *very closely*."

I'm not sure what she means by that. There's an odd gleam in her eye. "Oh, really?"

"Yeah, I had to keep up with how my boyfriend was doing."

"Oh, your boyfriend was in the contest? What's his name? Maybe I met him."

Erica tosses her head back and guffaws, revealing her perfectly straight, impeccably white teeth. When she's done cackling, she eyes me again and shakes her head, still giggling a little bit. "Don't be so silly. Jack is my boyfriend."

Twenty One

My heart, my stomach, my *everything* sinks. Completely sinks. My shoulders even slump down as I ignore my mama's voice in my head that's constantly nagging me to "stand up straight." It's like I've been punched right in the gut.

"Jack is your boyfriend?" I repeat, practically in a whisper.

"Well, yes and no. We broke up at the end of the school year, but we've been on and off since freshman year. I've been out of town a lot this summer, but now I'm back, so we're getting back together." As she talks, she admires herself in the mirror, running a brush through her golden hair and checking her makeup. "He's here tonight. I just saw him, but I haven't said hello yet."

"I know he's here. We came together," I shoot back, feeling defensive and territorial. What is wrong with me? Jack and I aren't a couple, but I'm getting all riled up. This girl ambushed me in the bathroom of all the doggone places. Unbelievable.

"Of course you did. Y'all make a great *singing* duo." Her tone has definitely turned snotty. She clears her throat and fake smiles at me in the mirror.

"Well, come on. Let's go see our guy." She flings her hair over her shoulder and heads for the door.

I haven't even peed yet, but I don't want her to have a head start. I'm not going to miss her reunion with Jack, no matter how sick to my stomach it makes me feel. Why didn't Jack ever mention her to me? He's been sort of flirty with me all this time, but maybe I misread the whole darn thing. That's what I get for listening to Hanna. She's always pushing me to go after boys, but boys keep secrets. I start to wonder what Ryder is hiding from her. This incident drives home the fact that we still don't know these boys all that well.

I follow closely behind Erica to join the crowded main floor of the club. She searches around for a few seconds before spotting "our guy" in the same location with Ryder, still enjoying the music and having no idea what's about to happen.

"There he is," Erica broadcasts when we inch closer to Jack and Ryder.

Jack notices her immediately. "Erica?" he asks in confusion but with a flicker of excitement in his eyes that makes my heart sink even further.

"Well, dagum. It's Erica Reynolds," Ryder chimes in.

"Hello, boys." She glances back and forth between them. "Is this any way to greet a lady?"

They each give her a hug while I remain behind her, incredibly out of place.

Jack comes back down to Earth and realizes I'm standing with them. "Oh, Erica, this is Olivia."

There's my full first name again.

She waves her hand in the air. "We already met. Let's get some fresh air, baby," she demands, grabbing his hand.

Ryder glances at me and shrugs, so we reluctantly follow them outside. I shouldn't go along, but my curiosity is getting the best of me. As long as Ryder is going, I figure I might as well trail them, too. Before we exit the club, I survey the area for Kat and Brett but don't see them. I can really use Kat's support right about now.

When I step onto the sidewalk just outside the door, I see Erica's arms and legs wrapped around Jack's body. She's squealing with delight that they're together again and saying how much she missed him. The Coke I just downed might come back up for an encore.

"So, you're back for good now?" Jack wonders.

I stand awkwardly beside Ryder, listening in as discreetly as possible.

"Sure am, baby. And I'm ready to pick up where we left off." She leans in to kiss Jack, but his eyes dart over to mine, and he pulls away.

"Maybe we should do this another time," he says in a low voice. "It's Ollie's birthday. We're here to celebrate that."

Erica glares at Jack with a mixture of hurt, disappointment, and anger written all over her face like she's about to pitch a fit. Instead, she reluctantly agrees, waving her hand with a frustrated sigh. "Fine."

Thankfully, we all head back inside. I spot Kat and Brett right away and rush over to them.

"Are you okay? You look strange." Kat gawks at me.

"I know why," Brett speaks up, pointing to Erica.

"Who's that?" she asks.

"Jack's girlfriend," I announce. The words feel foreign coming from my mouth. I'm still in shock.

Kat gasps, then Brett walks over to say hello to Erica.

The band tells the crowd that they're about to play their song, "Someone's Gonna Break Your Heart." I watch Erica, who appears to love being the center of attention, talk to Jack, Brett, and Ryder, laughing, batting her eyelashes, and flipping her hair. I realize how easily I've been replaced. The title of the song that's now blaring through the club rings true. Jack is that someone, except that he isn't going to break my heart because he already did.

Back in Jack's room, I lounge on his bed, staring up at the ceiling, wishing I hadn't gone in the bathroom at the club because then I wouldn't have met Erica. Well, I probably would have met her at some point, but maybe not on my birthday. We all left soon after she reunited with Jack. The rest of us headed home, but those two went God knows where to "catch up." Kat asked me if I wanted to stay with her and my mama tonight since she knew how upset

I was, but I said I wanted to be alone. It's worse than I thought, though, being by myself in his bedroom.

I'm just about to give up and go stay with them when I hear a faint knocking sound at the door. "Who's there?"

The door creaks open slowly, revealing Jack on the other side of it. "Did I wake you?"

"No," I reply flatly.

He steps inside the room and shuts the door behind him. Normally, this would get my heart rate up but not tonight. I'm numb. I can't even look at him. He lied to me. Well, he omitted a very big part of his life. How are we going to live together in Nashville if he's keeping secrets? Didn't he think Erica would show up sooner or later? Was he planning to keep this from me until then? The anger brews inside me. I fold my arms across my chest and glare straight ahead, refusing to acknowledge him any further.

"Something's wrong," he states. I don't say a word, so he continues. "You're sitting there pouting, so I know something's wrong."

"You think?" I finally look into his eyes. "How could you, Jack? Do you know how stupid I felt when she came up to me and said she's your girlfriend and I had no idea?"

"I'm sorry. I was going to tell you. Things with Erica are complicated." He glances down guiltily. "But I told her to back off since we were there for your birthday."

"But then we left early so you could go hang out with her!" I blurt out a little louder than I intend.

"You didn't want to be there, anyway. I saw your face fall when we got there."

"Don't blame this on me. You're a liar!"

"You never asked if I had a girlfriend!"

I put my hand up to stop him. "Don't shout at me."

"Besides," Jack says, using a calmer tone, "you and I just sing together. That's all."

I'm about to burst into tears, but so help me God, I will not let him see me cry over this. Over *him*. "Get out."

"You're kicking me out of my own room?"

"Get. Out."

Jack doesn't budge. He freezes right there, staring at me until I meet his eyes again. "I don't want you to leave tomorrow being upset with me. The next time we're together, we'll be moving into our townhouse in Nashville."

"Townhouse? What are you going on about?"

"Will called while I was out with—" Jack stops himself before bringing *her* name into this. "Well, anyway, Will called and said he got a place for us. We don't have to stay in a hotel like we thought."

"Oh. Wow," I manage, even more overwhelmed now.

Jack sits down next to me. "Ollie, I care about you a lot, but I can't guarantee who will or won't be in my life. We have to accept each other's friends and significant others for this partnership to work." He leans back and turns to face me. "I'll always be here for you. I'll always be your singing partner, if you'll let me."

I know he's right. He has a past, and I can't change that. I also know that his future may or may not include me, professionally or personally. Neither one of us has a crystal ball. But I'm still annoyed that he never mentioned Erica at all, especially since she's his high school sweetheart.

"Why didn't you tell me about her?"

"I didn't think it was important. We broke up."

"And now?" I bite my lip, wondering if they're back together.

There's an unmistakable somber expression on his face. "I have no idea. She's going to college here, and I'm moving away."

I feel kind of bad for him. I know what it's like to leave the people I care about the most behind. "I'm sorry I got so crazy. I was just surprised and hurt. I thought you were purposely keeping secrets from me."

Jack stretches his arms apart. "I'm an open book. It wasn't intentional." He tries a small smile. "Are we okay now?"

"I guess so."

"Good. You scared me a little bit when you told me to get out." He chuckles, and I join him.

When we stop laughing, the room falls silent for a few moments. It isn't awkward or uncomfortable, though. It's just me and Jack. Side by side.

"Do you love her?" I ask quietly.

He breathes in deeply, exhaling slowly. "I think I did," he replies eventually. "But things changed."

Somewhat relieved, I lay back on the bed, and Jack does the same.

After some quiet reflection, we turn on our sides to face each other. We lock eyes, and I feel like he can see inside me. Slowly, I inch closer to him, and he mirrors my movements. Our bodies almost touching, he takes my hand in his, our fingers tracing along every inch of each other's hands until they finally intertwine. We never break our eye contact.

My heart is thumping so hard that I wonder if he can hear it.

Then, Jack stops, still gazing at me with want in his eyes. "I should go," he whispers unconvincingly, much to my surprise. He jumps up before I can protest, and he's out the door in no time.

Adrenaline still pulsing through me, I stare at the indent on the comforter where his body was only seconds ago. Why did he take off like that? I don't know exactly what I wanted or expected to happen between us, but I wish he were here with me. I just want to be with him. Teardrops fall into my now lonely hand.

Worst birthday ever.

Twenty Two

One week later, I arrive at the Nashville airport by myself, absolutely terrified and unbelievably ecstatic to start this new journey. I decided to come to Nashville alone to get settled and then have Hanna, Kat, and my mama visit. They're anxiously waiting to see where I'll be living and what my new life will be like. I'm eager to see that, too.

Alyssa and Will arranged for a car to pick me up at the airport and bring me to the townhouse that I'll share with Jack. They didn't tell me much about it. All I have is my luggage and an address. On the way to the house, I decide to text message Jack to find out his whereabouts. He's driving here, so he'll have his truck with him. We haven't spoken at all in the past week, except for a few text messages. I'm nervous to see him again, but I hope we can forget about what happened, or didn't happen, on my birthday.

I'm on the way to the house.

It feels a little funny to call it "our house," so I stick with more general terms. Looking out at Nashville from the back of a Lincoln town car, I wait for his reply. This place is my new home. I get chill bumps just thinking about it. This is it. This is

Nashville. The city I've been dreaming about since I was a little girl. There are trees and green grass as far the eye can see. I can't wait to go downtown and become part of the music scene. I want to go to the honky-tonks and famous music venues that make this beautiful city legendary.

Just got here.

Jack is already there and gets to see everything first. I'm a little disappointed, but my delayed flight was out of my control. I just hope that he'll wait until I arrive to choose our bedrooms. Maybe batting my eyelashes and sweet talking him can get me the better room. It doesn't hurt to try. Besides, maybe he still feels a little bad about springing Erica on me out of the blue. I know I do, but I'm determined to move on.

When we reach the right address, I jump out of the car, spotting Jack's truck in the driveway. The house isn't brand new, but it doesn't look too old. There's a giant oak tree plopped right in the middle of the lawn. The brick exterior has white trimmed windows with forest green shutters. The driver helps me unload my bags and carry them up the front steps to the emerald door. I knock loudly, hoping Jack, Will, and Alyssa are still here since I don't have a key yet.

The door swings open, revealing Alyssa clad in jeans and a Belmont University t-shirt. "Welcome to Nashville!" she exclaims. "Come in. Come in." She waves her arm at me, motioning for me to step inside. "Will! Ollie is here!"

"There she is!" Will hollers, clapping his hands together. "How was the flight? Let me grab those for you." He gives me a half-hug, putting his arm around my shoulders quickly before walking past me to pick my bags up from the steps. He tips the driver and sends him on his way.

"Just fine. I've never flown before, so it was an adventure."

Alyssa raises her eyebrows in surprise. "Never, huh? Well, that was the first adventure of many!"

I smile, knowing that I'm about to experience a whole mess of new things. "I hope so."

"I know so," she assures me, nodding with an encouraging grin. "Jack's in the kitchen if you want to go see your new roomie."

"Yeah, he was starving, so he already dove into the groceries Alyssa picked up last night for you guys," Will explains.

I creep down the hall to the kitchen, admiring the hardwood floors and large windows that let the sunlight pour through. I like how cheerful the house is and the fact that it's fully furnished already, but I make a mental note to shop for some cool wall art.

When I enter the kitchen, I spy Jack sitting on the countertop, lathering up a piece of toast with peanut butter. His back is to me.

"Boo."

He twists around. "Hey, good lookin'. You made it." He hops off the counter and gives me the quickest hug ever.

I don't have any time to savor his scent or feel the warmth of his body on my skin. In that moment, I realize that I've missed him a lot in the week that we were apart. Much more so than I thought. "Yeah, here I am."

He settles on the counter again and continues eating his sandwich. "Want one? I'll paint some bread for you. Crunchy peanut butter with grape jelly's the best."

"Sure." I set my purse down on the floor and take a seat next to him. After removing my shoes, I watch Jack make a sandwich for me.

When it's ready, he hands it to me. "Here."

"Thanks, but it's kind of sloppy and lumpy."

"That means it's good."

I give him a sideways glance, both of us smiling. It seems that we've put the past behind us, and I'm grateful. The only sounds are of us chowing down on our food, until Will and Alyssa join us.

"You look right at home already," Alyssa notes, grinning as she eyes us perched on the kitchen counter with food spread out all around us, our bare feet dangling against the cabinets. "I know you both probably want to unpack, but we have some business to take care of first."

I raise my eyebrows while Jack simply nods in response to Alyssa.

"Yeah, we need to pick a name for your duo," Will tells us. "Something simple, yet catchy and a little less boring than just Jack and Ollie."

"Something *country*," Alyssa emphasizes.

We all gather at the kitchen table, and Alyssa grabs a pen and paper out of the organizer she always carries with her.

"Let's jot down some ideas," she suggests.

Crickets. No one makes a sound. It's like we're back in high school, avoiding the teacher's request for volunteers.

Finally, Will clears his throat. "How about we combine your names somehow?"

Jack and I shrug in response.

"I like that idea. What do you guys think of Jallie?" Alyssa asks.

Jack perks up, but not in a good way. "Nope. Way too girly sounding. There's a guy in this duo. Let's not forget." He motions for Alyssa to hand the paper and pen to him, so she slides it over. "What about Olack?"

I groan. "That's worse than Jallie."

"Let's try your last names combined," Will offers. "Kennley?"

"I kind of like that," I admit, mulling it over. Then, it hits me. "Wait a minute. What do y'all think of Adlenna? When you say it fast, it sort of sounds like Atlanta, especially with a Southern accent. Atlanta's where everything started for us."

Jack's eyes light up. "I love it."

We high five, then turn to Will and Alyssa. The looks on their faces say it all.

"Perfect," they agree in unison.

Jack and I pick our rooms, and I try to settle in. It doesn't feel like home yet, and I'm a bundle of nerves. I begin unpacking my pink leopard luggage. The silence is way too loud. And lonely. There's only one thing that will make me feel better. Singing. I listened to Miranda Lambert's albums on the way here, including her trio Pistol Annie's album. "Lemon Drop" is the song rattling around in my head, so I belt it out while I fold clothes and put them in the closet and drawers. Luckily, Jack and I don't have to do too much in the way of decorating. But maybe that's why it doesn't feel like home. Mama will bring more of my belongings when she visits, so I have no doubt that I'll fill up all the space soon enough. I continue singing and getting used to my surroundings as best I can.

"Beautiful."

I whip my head around to see Jack in the doorway. I furrow my brow in confusion. "My room?"

"Your voice." He chuckles for a second. "Obviously."

"Oh," I reply, glancing away shyly. "So…"

Jack shoves his hands in his pockets. "What do you want to do now?"

I think of my conversation with Hannah about kissing Jack and feel a flash of embarrassment. I hope it doesn't show. "I don't know," I answer cautiously.

"We should probably listen to those songs Will and Alyssa left for us. You know, get a feel for them."

"Good idea," I agree.

We go into the living room and practice our songs for a couple hours until we get restless. It's then that Jack suggests we work on our own music, so I take my laptop out, and he grabs his guitar. We toss around some ideas, various melodies and lyrics, and after a while of just messing around, we decide to buckle down and write our next song. Once we focus, the music and lyrics flow naturally, just like they did at the lake and at Jack's parents' house.

"You want to order a pizza?" Jack asks. "I'm starving."

"This last verse can be better. Let's work on it some more before we eat." My eyes are starting to blur from staring at the computer screen, but the lyrics still need some tweaking.

"Fine," he says, "but I do need to take a bathroom break." He puts his guitar down and disappears down the hall.

While he's gone, I finish the lyrics. "Got it!" I shout.

When Jack reenters the room, I tell him to play the song, so we can sing along and make sure everything is how we want it.

We high-five when we finish performing the song to an empty room. I imagine hearing it on the radio for the first time and singing it for sold-out crowds. There's so much that can happen. So much potential.

"Now, let's eat," I announce, getting to my feet. "Why don't we go out and explore the city a little bit?" I give Jack a mischievous grin. "Let's get into some trouble."

"You want to be a troublemaker now?" He raises his eyebrows, a teasing smile forming on his lips.

I nod. "Yes, sir."

He walks toward me with that playful twinkle in his eyes. "Nobody loves trouble as much as me."

We share a flirtatious smile, both of us blushing, before heading to our rooms to get ready.

Two Voices
Written by Jack Bradley and Ollie McKenna

Saw you standing there
Without a care
Blue-eyed boy, shy smile
I talked. You listened.

Georgia peach in front of me
Your spirit so free
Blue-eyed girl, bright smile
I listened. You talked.

On and on and on

Two hearts with a dream
Two voices with a song
Just you and me
Yeah, you and me
God brought us here
Together without fear

I've been thinking
And I've been thinking, too
We're better together
Yeah, you and me

Two hearts with a dream
Two voices with a song
Just you and me
Yeah, you and me

God brought us here
Together without fear

You can rely on me
And you can rely on me, too
Trust me. Yeah, trust me

Two hearts with a dream
Two voices with a song
Just you and me
Yeah, you and me
God brought us here
Together without fear

Two voices with a song

Twenty Three

Third wheel. Ugh. While Jack and I were fixing to leave, there was a knock at the door. Brett had an argument with his parents about college, so he hopped on a plane to Nashville. Jack and I haven't even spent one night alone together in our new place. But that's probably for the best, although I do want to see what living with just Jack is like. Oh well. We didn't explore the city like Jack had suggested. Instead, we brought pizza back home, and the boys set up the Xbox to play video games all night. After two boring hours of watching them play, I call it a night and go to my room. This evening sure turned out to be one heck of a letdown. I have Brett to thank for that.

"Yeah. He just showed up here a few hours ago," I tell Kat when I call her. "I had no idea he was coming."

"That's…odd," she replies, her voice sounding as weird as Brett's unexpected visit.

"What do you know?" I can sense from her hesitance that she's keeping something from me. "Spill it, Kat."

"It's nothing. Honest."

"If there's one thing you're not being, it's honest. Tell me what's going on right now or I'll call Mama."

I know it's a childish, empty threat, but since Kat is so far away, I don't have much of a choice. She could just hang up on me and that would be that. I'm discovering the disadvantages of being away from home.

"Oh, Ollie, it's just that…" Her voice trails off, then she draws in a long breath, letting it out in a frustrated huff. "I knew Brett was going to see y'all. Okay? Happy now?"

I plop down on my bed with a thump and crinkle my brow. "I don't get it. He told you, but not us?"

"Ask Jack."

"Ask Jack what?"

"Just ask him why Brett's there."

"Brett already told us that he had an argument with his parents."

Kat sighs. "If you're going to be in the music business, of all industries, you have to learn to question everything. Don't be so easily fooled."

"What in the world are you going on about? I'm lost," I admit.

"Oh, for Pete's sake, Ollie. Jack asked Brett to visit as soon as possible," she blurts out. "No fight with his family. None of that." She sighs again. "There. You got me to tell you."

I shake my head. "But…" Confusion and disappointment weigh me down. "I don't understand."

"Looks like he's getting cold feet again. Just do everything you can to get in front of some record label executives with Jack. Once they see you, I know they'll be hooked, even if you want to move forward without Jack."

"Huh? Without Jack?"

"I gotta go. Sutter's here. Talk soon. Love you," she says in a hurry, then clicks off.

What the heck just happened? Here I am again, feeling like the rug has been ripped out from under me, just like that night at the restaurant when Jack said he'd rather be a solo artist. Is he really having second thoughts and that's why he told Brett to come here? Why can't Jack just talk to me about it? Why is he always pushing me away? We're supposed to be in this together.

Enough is enough. I storm out of my room and into the living room where Jack and Brett are still engrossed in those stupid games.

"Jack," I croak out, trying to maintain my nerve to confront him. "I need to talk to you."

"Okay," he says over his shoulder, not even glancing my way.

"Alone," I clarify. "Right now," I demand, raising my voice.

He finally turns around, meets my eyes, and his face drops. He knows something isn't right. "Let's go out to my truck."

We head outside, walking barefoot across the lawn, and climb into the bed of Jack's pickup, sitting down opposite each other.

"Nice night," he mumbles.

He's right. The hot night air feels good on my skin, not quite as humid and sticky as Georgia's summer nights. But I don't want to chat about the weather.

After I don't respond, his face scrunches up with concern. "So, what's up?"

I stay quiet, not really knowing exactly what to say or how to say it. After a few minutes of uncomfortable silence, I lock eyes with him. "Why are you afraid of me?"

He tosses his head back in surprise and laughs. "Afraid of you? You dragged me outside to ask me a silly question like that?"

Silly. That's what Erica called me. My stomach churns. I want to run back inside, pack my bags, and go home. But then I remember that he's in the wrong here. He should be embarrassed for calling Brett.

"Why is Brett here tonight?"

"He told you already. He was arguing with—" He stops when I put my hand up.

"Don't you lie to me."

Jack glances down, fidgeting with his hands. "You know I asked him here?" He searches my face for confirmation, so I nod once. "Sorry, Ollie. I should have told you."

"Why do you want him here so soon?" I wonder. "We've barely had any time to rehearse on our own. I can't imagine that you're homesick already. This is only the first night."

"I just don't know if we should be living together…alone. I've never lived with a girl before. Well, except for my mom, but that's different." He gives me a shy smile. "I don't know if I'm ready for this arrangement," he admits, taking a deep breath. "So, if it's okay with you, Brett has agreed to stay with us for the rest of the summer until school starts." He raises his eyebrows, waiting for my response, then adds, "It would make things a little easier on me, so I could focus more on our music."

I have to admit that he's good. Jack knows exactly what to say to get me to cave in. He knows I want the music to be our number one priority. I'm not exactly thrilled about adding another boy to the mix, but Brett is pretty cool, and if his presence will benefit Jack and ultimately help us concentrate on our music...

"Fine," I agree. I'm just glad he's being honest with me and confessed his insecurity about our new situation that doesn't involve not wanting to sing with me. Even though Brett is here, it seems like Jack and I can still get closer.

"Great," he says with a relieved grin. "Thanks, Ollie. I'm gonna head back in and tell Brett the good news." He takes off before I can say anything else.

And now I'll have to tell my mama that I'm living with *another* boy. Lord, have mercy.

Twenty Four

What my mama doesn't know won't bother her. That's why I've decided not to mention Brett's new address to her, and I made sure that he and Kat know to keep their mouths shut, too. Lying isn't very becoming of anyone, but I consider it just omitting a fact. Besides, my mama and Kat aren't coming to visit until after Jack and I record our demo.

For two weeks, we rehearse, record, and repeat steps one and two. We're on a roll, and Will and Alyssa agree to let us record the two songs we wrote ourselves. We're over the moon about that. Brett comes with us to the studio most of the time. He's actually really helpful, bringing me tea and anything I need to make the process easier. Jack was right. It's nice having him around, and his company has prevented any awkward moments between me and Jack so far.

Everything is moving along nicely, and we're all having a good time, despite the fast pace and pressures of securing a showcase with record labels. If our demo generates enough interest, Jack and I can perform for the record executives who want to hear us sing live, which can then lead to signing with one of their labels, if they like us. I want that showcase so bad that I can practically taste it.

The morning after a long recording session that went into the wee hours, I bolt upright after a nightmare that Jack and I were performing for the record labels and my voice was gone. I tried, but I couldn't make a sound. I had let everyone down. Now, I'm perched on the edge of my bed, reminding myself to breathe. My throat is parched, and I'm sweating all over. Never in my life have I felt so overwhelmed. The stakes are high. This isn't only about trying to make my own career happen anymore. I'm responsible for Jack's dreams coming true, too. The pressure is like an elephant sitting on my shoulders that I can't ignore. Then, there's a knock on my door.

"Ollie?"

"Yeah?" I whisper.

Jack carefully opens it and steps inside. "The truck's ready to go."

I stare at him, dumbfounded. "Ready to go where?" I glance at the clock on my nightstand. "We don't have rehearsal until tonight. I want to get some more shut eye for a few hours." That isn't likely with all the worries plaguing me, but I hope that maybe the sheer exhaustion will overcome all those incessant thoughts that gnaw at me.

"No rehearsal tonight," he says simply.

"What?"

"I cleared the night with Will and Alyssa. We're off." He smiles triumphantly, motioning with his head as he beckons me to get up.

I rise to my feet, but don't move any closer to him. "We can't take time off, Jack. We just got here. We have a lot of work to do."

"Just trust me. It's okay."

"It's not okay. We need to keep going."

"We will. Tomorrow. Tonight, we're free." He grins again.

I tilt my head skeptically. "I don't know if this is best."

Jack lets out a long sigh. "Well, I'm not working tonight, so you don't really have a choice. We're in this together, remember?"

I hesitate, then nod. "Yeah."

"Get your shoes on. We're heading out."

"Is Brett coming, too?"

"Nope. Just you and me." He raises his eyebrows before swiftly disappearing down the hallway.

After changing into a T-shirt and jean shorts and rushing to put some makeup on, I grab a pair of sneakers and some sandals. I'm not sure which will be more appropriate since I don't know where we're going. Can we actually have a carefree day off? It doesn't seem possible at this point, but I'll sure give it a try. Jack revs his truck up, so I scurry to the door, saying goodbye to Brett, who's in the kitchen eating a bowl of cereal, as I pass by. When I get in, Jack and I exchange excited smiles, and then we're off on another adventure.

♫

On the highway, our windows are down and the music is blaring. Country music, of course. I still have no idea what our destination will be, but I decide to trust Jack and let him take me where he wants to.

About four hours later, Jack and I reach Tupelo, Mississippi, and pull into a gas station. We sang along to the radio the whole way down here, my bare feet up on the dashboard, and our hands waving through the summer air. I'm a little sad that the road trip is over. Jack told me that Tupelo is Elvis's birthplace, and he's been wanting to visit for a long time.

"For you," Jack says, appearing at the car door after he fills the tank. He's holding a wildflower out to me.

"Where'd you get that?" I wonder, a giddy smile spreading across my face.

"Just over there. Off the side of the road." He leans in, and I inch closer to him.

I extend my hand to take the flower, but he puts it in my hair instead. We both laugh at the exact same time.

"Thank you," I whisper. "It's real pretty."

Jack nods. "So are you."

Blushing like crazy, I lean back. Jack jumps in, starts the engine, and we're off again. This time, we're headed to the house where Elvis was born.

We spend time at the museum near the shotgun house where Elvis began his life, then walk around the park and visit the church. The whole area is very serene and totally relaxing. Even though we're visiting a place dedicated to The King of Rock 'n Roll, I manage to forget about my own budding music career for a couple hours. All I want to do is soak up the legacy of a music legend. Jack asks the people working there a bunch of questions about Elvis and chats up other strangers who are visiting, just like us. I see the same spark in his eye here as I did when he was on the baseball field and the night we wrote our first song together. Jack is a laidback guy most of the time, but I love watching his enthusiasm come out just like a little kid on Christmas morning.

The next stop on our Tupelo adventure is Johnnie's Drive-In, a town staple where Elvis used to hang out. Jack wants to sit in the same booth where Elvis used to dine, but it's already taken. After our cheap, greasy hamburgers and fries, we drive up and down Main Street. I stick my head out the window and take pictures of the Elvis-themed guitar sculptures that line the sidewalks. We wind up at the site of the old fairgrounds where Elvis gave his "Welcome Home" concert in the 1950s. It's now a park with a huge fountain in front of City Hall.

"You think we'll ever have concerts in our hometowns?" I ask Jack after we make our way over to the swing set and each take a seat.

"Hope so," he replies with a shrug.

I kick my legs out just a little bit to get the swing going. "Me, too."

For a few serene minutes, we take in the historic Tupelo scenery around us. Without any warning, my eyes well with tears, and it isn't long before they spill out onto my cheeks. I have no idea why I'm crying.

"Hey," Jack whispers, gently touching my arm in response to my sniffling. "What's wrong?"

"I don't know," I croak out. That nightmare sweeps through my head again, and the tears come with even more force. "I don't want to disappoint you. I don't want to let anyone down."

He turns his swing to face mine, the chains twisting. "What are you talking about?"

"There's just so much pressure." I gasp for air. "*So much.*"

"You're only making it worse for yourself. You gotta remember why we're doing this." He raises his eyebrows at me, but when I don't respond, he continues. "We just want to share our music with other people. And we're going to do that the best we can. That's all there is to it."

I manage to let out a brief laugh, even though I was blubbering like a baby just a few moments ago. "You make it sound so easy."

"I'm not saying there won't be hard work. We have a mountain to climb to be heard by a lot of people, but we have to stay focused on that. We want to be heard. Everything else is just gravy." He nods, and I'm glad at least one of us is so sure. Jack's levelheadedness is truly the foundation of Adlenna because I'm still a mess.

"I wouldn't want to do any of this without you," I confess in a soft, shy voice.

Jack grabs my hand and weaves his fingers between mine, a wonderful, yet unexpected show of affection that reminds me of the fleeting moment we shared together on my birthday. From the spark in his eyes, I know he remembers it, too.

"Ditto."

We tear our eyes away from each other and stare into the distance, still holding onto the moment by holding onto each other.

Jack's skin feels electrifying against mine, and our fingers fit just right together, like pieces of a puzzle.

"Do you want to stay the night here?" he asks, almost inaudibly.

I hesitate for a few seconds. "Okay."

That night, Jack and I get a quick bite to eat near the hotel where we reserved a cheap room. We decided it would be better to rent only one room to save money, but that didn't stop me from being embarrassed when the desk clerk eyed us curiously, booking our room with a knowing look like he suspected what would happen between me and Jack.

"We're adults," I had blurted out, even though no one asked, and it wasn't any of his business. But I didn't like the way he was judging us. Little did he know, Jack and I were already living together. I thought about adding that, but figured it was best to keep it to myself and ignore his creepy leer.

After dinner, Jack and I head up to the room where, thankfully, there are two double beds. I keep wondering if the guy at the front desk was on to something. Is Jack going to make a move? He had seemed so against us getting involved beyond our friendship and professional partnership. He *did* hold my hand at the park, though. But what about Erica? Isn't he still into her? It seemed like it on my birthday. In any case, I'm nervous. So much for the peaceful day we had.

Some uneasy silence ensues as we settle into the room. I choose the bed closest to the window, and Jack claims the bed closest to the door. We both have immediate ways to flee the awkward scene, though mine is a bit more of a challenge since we're on the second floor.

"Look, we get free movies," Jack announces after taking a seat on his bed and flipping the TV on from the remote secured to the nightstand.

"We don't get these channels at home." I pause. "At my house in Summerville, I mean."

"We don't get them at our place in Nashville either," he adds. He called it "our place," which covers my body in chill bumps. The good kind.

Relaxing on my bed to watch TV with Jack, I'm soon shocked by the images on the screen that turn my face red instantly. I can't even look at Jack. We're watching a graphic sex scene. How did that happen? It seems like it's going in slow motion, and we're both too frozen to do anything about it. My mama would kill me if she knew what I was seeing. I can't believe my eyes, or my ears. It's so *embarrassing*, yet educational. They don't teach you about this kind of stuff in school, that's for darn sure. I hear Jack fumbling for the remote, then the TV goes dark.

"Uh," he starts, "I'm exhausted. Time to hit the hay." He bolts for the bathroom, and I hear the faucet turn on.

We had picked up some toothpaste and toothbrushes in the little shop in the lobby.

I don't know what to do with myself, so I grab the notepad on the table and the pen next to it.

Jack walks out of the bathroom a few minutes later, and slips into bed. "Night, Ollie," he mumbles.

"Goodnight," I mutter in response.

It's official. The guy downstairs was wrong. Nothing romantic is going to happen between me and Jack. But I know I still won't be able to get much sleep, so I turn my attention to the sheets of paper instead and frantically scribble down the lyrics that are bursting out of me.

Hooked On You
Written by Ollie McKenna

It wasn't much, but I fell for your touch
You're like a sweet smelling perfume
And fresh flowers in my room
The way you get me makes me swoon

I'm hooked on how you say my name
And how you drive your truck
When we lock eyes, I know I'm in luck
I'm hooked on how you throw a baseball real far
And the way you play guitar
Oh, I'm hooked on you

I like it when you're at my door
You know just what to say
That makes me want you even more
You're my guy, I hope and pray

I'm hooked on how you say my name
And how you drive your truck
When we lock eyes, I know I'm in luck
I'm hooked on how you throw a baseball real far
And the way you play guitar
Oh, I'm hooked on you

You set the hook
I took the bait
You're reeling me in
But is it just a game?

I'm hooked on how you say my name
And how you drive your truck
When we lock eyes, I know I'm in luck
I'm hooked on how you throw a baseball real far
And the way you play guitar
Oh, I'm hooked on you

Twenty Five

Jack and I get an early start the following morning. We're on the road by seven o'clock after grabbing some coffee and doughnuts from the free breakfast at the hotel. Neither of us say anything about the day or night before. Well, we do chat about how cool it was to see all the Elvis sites, but everything from the hand holding at the park to the awkwardness in our room seems to be off limits.

Aside from a few stops for bathroom breaks and to fill the tank, we make great time and arrive back in Nashville around noon. I can't wait to take a shower, get into some clean clothes, and get ready for the studio. Tonight, Jack and I will be finishing our demo, and I'm definitely anxious, but in a good way. After seeing how Elvis started from such humble beginnings and defied the odds to become a music icon, both of us are even more inspired. I'm itching to wrap the demo up and find out where it might take us. The time is now. Nothing can stand in our way.

When we reach our house, I practically race inside, but stop short when I see who's in the living room with Brett.

"Mama? Kat?" I sputter. "What are you doing here?"

"Well, good afternoon to you too, baby," my mama answers, her words clipped and her forehead creased.

Something is wrong. That much I know. Kat won't make eye contact with me, but it's Mama's intense stare that gives it away. She's upset. I'm definitely familiar with that look. Maybe she knows that I watched a few minutes of a dirty movie last night. But why would she come all this way to scold me over a stupid movie? I'm old enough to watch whatever I want.

Jack bursts through the door, but halts in his tracks just like I did. "Miss Jolene. Kat. What a surprise." He shoots a curious look my way, but I just shrug in response. At this point, I know as much about their visit as he does.

"Well, what brings y'all here? I told you I'd let you know once we finished the demo, and then y'all could come see us. We aren't quite done yet." All I want to do is chill out before our last recording session, but no. That isn't happening with an annoyed Mama plopped on my couch.

"I drove down here to witness for myself what's really going on," my mama confesses, glaring back and forth between me and Jack.

"You don't trust us?" I ask in disbelief. I hadn't forgotten to call or at least text her every day since we moved. Why am I being punished?

"No, I do not, Olivia Myrtle McKenna." *Uh oh.* She used my full name, which definitely means trouble.

"Myrtle?" Jack tries to stifle a laugh.

My eyes flash to his and that shuts him up real fast.

"You deceived me," my mama continues. "I told you that moving here was okay as long as you kept me involved. But you've been fudging the truth, missy."

Kat drops her head to her hands. "I'm sorry, Ollie. I'd just had a fight with Sutter. I was angry, so I blurted it out to her. I'm really sorry."

"And I wonder how you found out," Jack interjects as all eyes shift to Brett.

"Uh, I should go. This seems like a family matter," Brett blurts out, trying to escape.

"I think you're right," Jack agrees, seizing the opportunity to skedaddle, too.

They both dart out the front door in a flash. *Thanks for nothing, boys.*

"I haven't been fibbing," I explain. "He's only been here a couple weeks, and I didn't want to worry you. He's been Jack's best friend for years. He's practically family. It's no big deal."

My explanation only seems to enrage my mama even more as she scrambles to her feet in a huff.

"How could you think it's no big deal to live with not one, but *two* boys?" she asks in a booming voice. "I knew I shouldn't have let you do this."

"I hate to be the one to point this out, but Ollie's grown now. You don't really have a say." Kat probably came to my defense since she's feeling guilty about telling on me.

"That's enough, Kat," my mama declares in a calmer yet stern tone. "I don't like this one bit. Not one bit."

"Brett's a nice boy. He's respectful, and he's been really helpful to have around while Jack and I have been so busy. He's a good guy." I stare directly at her, refusing to back down. "Please don't ruin this or make it more difficult than it already is."

Her expression softens, and she sits down again. "I suppose I can allow it. But I'm going to stick around for a little while to keep an eye on y'all."

"What about your store?" I know Jack isn't going to be thrilled to have my family here all the time since we're already in close quarters, but I let Brett stay, so it's only fair.

"Granddaddy will check in on it, and the girls working there will get along just fine without me."

"How long is a little while?"

"Hey, don't push it. I'll decide when it's time for me to leave."

My stomach stirs with frustration. "We don't really have room for y'all here."

"Don't you dare say that your own mother and sister aren't welcome in your home." Her eyes are like daggers again, so I know I'm rocking the boat.

"That's not what I meant." I sigh. There's no way out of this. "Y'all can share my room. I'll sleep out here."

"No. You and Kat share your room. I'll take the living room."

But this is where we all hang out and where Jack and Brett play video games. I whip my phone out of my pocket to text Jack.

Mama & Kat are staying. Can Mama have Brett's room? She refuses to take my room...wants to squat in the living room...

Within seconds he replies.

Yeah. That's fine with him.

Brett has been staying on the couch in the extra room that is set up like an office, but it's better than my mama planting herself in the main room of the house and sticking her nose in everyone's business at all hours.

I share the good news with her, and Brett's "generosity" scores him some brownie points. Win-win.

Mama retreats to Brett's room, and I'm relieved that she's out of my hair. She has already seen my room anyway. She snooped around before I even got home and helped herself to a tour of the house. I love her, but I don't like the way she ambushed me with this extended visit. Honestly, she gets under my skin, coming here without any warning and accusing me of being a liar.

"What happened with Sutter?" I ask Kat when we get to my room alone.

"You promise not to tell?" Kat pleads, a sense of urgency in her voice as she closes the door.

"I guess so, but maybe I'll just blurt it out when I'm angry," I tease, only sort of meaning it.

"Ollie. This is serious." A strange expression crosses over her face, so I sit down.

"I'm all ears."

She paces around my room, fidgeting with the hairband around her wrist. "I don't know how to say this." Her breathing is shallow, and her eyes are bugged out like she's really scared.

"Just spit it out," I urge her, trying to sound calm, even though she's really starting to shake me up.

Kat turns away from me to tell whatever it is to the wall instead. "I think I'm pregnant."

I'm at a loss for words, which is extremely rare for me. Did I hear correctly? Did my older sister who always has everything so together really just tell me that her whole life might be changing forever? How can this be happening?

"I…I don't know what to say…"

"That's a first."

"I know." I take a few deep breaths, trying to calm down and make some sense of this. "You aren't sure?"

She faces me. "I took three tests at home. Two were positive, and one was negative."

"You need to go to a doctor." I can see the fear in her eyes, so I reach out and grab her hand. "I'll go with you, if you want." I pause for a second. "Why doesn't Sutter want to go with you and know for certain? I'm guessing the fight was about this, right?"

"Not exactly." Her face turns darker shades of pink by the second. "I did tell him that I might be pregnant, but that's not why he's mad." She inhales sharply, her face and neck tense. "He pitched a fit because if it's true, and I really am pregnant, he isn't the father."

My mouth drops open. "What are you talking about? You cheated on Sutter? I don't believe it." I tilt my head in doubt. "Then who is?"

Kat won't look me in the eye again. "Brett," she reveals in a faint whisper.

I gasp. "No way!"

"That's why I didn't want to come here, but Mama insisted on dragging me along." She focuses on me with desperation in her eyes. "Please, Ollie. Promise you won't say anything to anyone."

"I promise," I reluctantly agree. "But you have to promise me that you'll find out for sure as soon as possible."

"I'll go later today to one of those urgent care places that take walk-ins."

"But I have to go to the studio. I can't go with you."

Kat waves her hand. "It's okay. That's actually perfect because we can tell Mama that I'm going to the studio with you. She won't suspect a thing."

"Unless she wants to come with us, too." I stop for a second to think. "No, I'll just tell her that Jack and I really need to focus tonight, and we can't have any distractions."

"Good." She squeezes my hand. "Thank you."

"You sure you'll be okay on your own?"

Kat lets out a weak, strained laugh. "If I'm pregnant, I'll have to get used to being on my own. Sutter will leave me for sure." Her eyes fill with tears. "I really messed up. I'm so stupid."

"Don't say that. You aren't stupid." I don't know how much she wants to tell me, but I decide to go ahead anyway. "So, when did you and Brett...you know? I thought y'all hated each other."

"Hate is a strong word." Kat stands up and walks over to my dresser. "It happened in Atlanta in the back of my Jeep. It's so sleazy, I know. But I'm not usually like that, I swear. It's just that Brett is different... he makes me feel differently than Sutter does. It's hard to explain."

"You and Sutter have been together a long time."

"Too long, I guess. Maybe I was bored, and that's why I let it go too far with Brett. Just wanted to know what it was like to be with someone else for a change."

"Do you... Do you like Brett?" It's hard for me to imagine them as a couple.

All this time, it's seemed like she belongs with Sutter. But maybe we're all wrong. She's been pushing him away lately, but I figured she'd come around. She always goes back to Sutter. But maybe now, he won't go back to her.

"Brett's okay." That's all she offers on the subject.

"Just okay? There had to be something more for you to go all the way with him."

Kat breathes an angry sigh. "I told you I was bored."

"If you're bored, you go to the mall, or watch TV, or take a walk. You don't cheat on your boyfriend with a guy you despise just for kicks." I guess I'm getting riled up now because I'm sad for her. Even though she's the older sister, I feel protective over her, and I don't want to see her in any pain.

"You don't understand!" She starts sobbing.

I hurry over to her and put my arm around her. "I'm sorry. I'll back off." I pause while she wipes her eyes. "I'm going to take a shower. Maybe a nap will help you feel a little better," I suggest.

"Good idea," she agrees.

I start off for the bathroom.

"Ollie?" she calls out.

I turn around. "Yeah?"

"I'm really thankful we're sisters." The tiniest of grins sweeps across her mouth, and then it's gone.

I smile in return. "Me, too."

Twenty Six

"Ollie, pull back at the end of the second line of the bridge, so Jack's voice can take over for the next line. It'll be a better sounding transition between your voices," our producer, Kevin, instructs me. He's been hard at work with me and Jack for the past four hours. "Ready to try it again?"

I adjust my headphones and give him two thumbs up from inside the booth. It's such a thrill to record music professionally, and to top it all off, we're working on "Two Voices," one of the songs Jack and I wrote together. I lock eyes with Jack who's waiting patiently beside me at the next microphone.

He gives me a comforting grin. "Let's do it."

The track plays, and we sing the bridge again.

"Nailed it," Kevin assures us. "We got it. Onward."

Will and Alyssa are hanging out in the control room with Kevin and a few other people who I don't recognize. They showed up after Jack and I already went into the booth. One of the guys is really cute. He has short, blonde hair and dazzling, blue eyes that really draw my attention. He's chatting with Will and Alyssa, and I can't help but notice the adorable way he laughs. I *have* to meet him.

When we wrap "Two Voices," Jack and I exit the booth and join everyone else. We get a round of applause and high fives from Kevin, Will, and Alyssa. Everyone seems really pleased with the work we've done. It's been a really long night, but the demo is finally done. It still has to be mastered, but that is Kevin's and his team's responsibility. He guarantees Will and Alyssa that it will be ready to send out in a couple days. No one wants to waste any time because they want to capitalize on the bit of notoriety Jack and I received from Atlanta Idol and keep the buzz going.

Alyssa approaches us with the blonde guy in tow. "Jack, Olivia, I want to introduce you to one of the artists whose career we're also managing. This is Colt Carson."

Jack shakes his hand first. "Nice to meet you."

"You, too," Colt responds as he lets go of Jack's hand and turns to me. He gently takes my hand in his and kisses the top of it.

I giggle. "What a gentleman. Your mama raised you right. Pleasure to meet you."

"The pleasure's all mine," he says, winking.

"What kind of music do you sing?" Jack wonders, interrupting my moment with Colt.

"Christian rock. I'm a singer-songwriter, and I play guitar." He smiles confidently at both of us. He's gorgeous.

"Cool," Jack responds flatly.

"You guys sounded amazing tonight. Your demo is killer. I love country music," Colt continues.

"Around these parts you kind of have to love it," I tell him with another little giggle.

He nods in agreement. "Hey, I know it's late, but do y'all want to grab something to eat? There's a café nearby that's open twenty-four hours. What do you say?" Colt glances eagerly between me and Jack, but he mostly makes eye contact with me.

Jack clears his throat. "Thanks, but I don't think so. We've been working all night, and we're exhausted."

"Yeah, I'm tired, but I still want to go. You don't have to come if you don't want to, Jack." From the stunned look on his face, I gather that he didn't expect me to accept Colt's offer. But I figure, why not? I probably wouldn't have jumped at a chance like this before Atlanta, but things are changing. I like meeting new people more now, especially boys, and stepping outside my comfort zone.

"Uh, okay. Y'all have a good time."

"Thanks, man. See you around," Colt says as he turns his attention to me. "Let's go, Olivia."

"You can call me Ollie. All my friends do."

He grins. "We're friends already?"

"I hope so," I respond, blushing. "My mama wouldn't want me going out with a boy I hardly know."

"Then we're definitely friends," he confirms with another teasing smile. "Come on." He wraps his arm around me, and we head for the door.

Behind me I can hear Alyssa telling Jack, "Don't worry. He's a great guy. Let her go."

♫

"I knew you were from Georgia," I say to Colt after he tells me he's from Macon in my home state.

We snag a table and start in on our Cokes and pepperoni pizza.

"Yeah, born and bred in the Heart of Georgia." He flashes that devilish grin again. "I actually know a few people who tried out for Atlanta Idol this year, but they didn't make it past the preliminaries." He lowers his head, looking shy.

"What is it?"

"I voted for you," Colt admits.

An unstoppable smile spreads across my face. "Really?"

"I followed along the whole way. I just had to do my part to help the most beautiful girl I had ever seen reach her dream." He's really turning on the charm now. His shy moment passed right quick. "And I have to admit that I was happier than a pig in mud when Will and Alyssa signed you. I'm glad they took my advice."

"Your advice?" I inquire, puzzled.

"I told them that they needed to go see an amazing girl in the Atlanta Idol competition. And they told me they were planning to check out the finals, anyway, but I like to think my recommendation gave them that extra push." He beams at me.

"Well, thank you," I respond, extremely flattered. "You're too kind." I take a sip of Coke. "When did you meet Will and Alyssa?"

Colt finishes chewing the bite of pizza he just took and swallows. "I moved here about two years ago, and not long after I arrived, they snatched me up when I was playing a gig downtown."

"They sure know how to pick 'em. I haven't heard your music yet, but I trust that it's awesome."

"Stop it. You're making me blush," he teases.

We both laugh, then continue chatting. The conversation is so easy. Colt is a real gem, good looking, sweet, funny, and talented. I lose track of the time since we're having so much fun, but when I pull out my phone, I see ten new text messages and that it's almost four in the morning. From all the excitement at the studio when we were recording, and my semi-date with Colt, I plum forgot to check in with Kat. She was supposed to see a doctor. Most of the messages are from her.

I'm going away for a few days. Need to clear my head.

Please don't tell Mama. Cover for me, okay?

Ollie, are you there? Tell Mama I went to stay with a friend nearby.

If you make anything up on your own, be sure to tell me so we get our stories straight.

I'm sorry if this gets you into any trouble.

I love you.

What does all that mean? Kat didn't say if she's pregnant or not. How can she not tell me the truth and just disappear like this? Is she really with a friend? I don't think she has any friends around here. Mama will be furious if she finds out what's going on. Why is Kat putting me in this position? Is she pregnant?

The next two messages are from Hanna.

What's going on with Kat? Rumors are spreading…

I went by your house, but no one's there. Where are Kat and your mama?

It must have slipped my mind to tell Hanna that Mama and Kat are with me in Nashville. Well, only my mama now. It sounds like word is getting around town back home that something isn't right. Did Sutter spill the beans? He's the only one who knows, isn't he? Kat didn't mention where their fight was. Maybe people overheard. Doggone it. Where the heck is she now?

The last two messages are from Jack.

Are you okay? It's real late.

I'm not waiting up anymore. Get home safe.

He was waiting up for me? Why? His last message was received at two thirty six. He stayed up that late? I don't have time to think about it. I have to write back to Kat.

Where are you? Are you pregnant? Are you okay? When will I see you?

I stare at the screen after I hit send, waiting anxiously, but wherever she is, she's probably sleeping now.

"Everything alright?" Colt asks, jerking me back to reality.

"Yeah," I lie. "Forgot to check my phone all night."

"Having too much fun, right?"

"Exactly." I'm ready to leave. Those texts put a sour taste in my mouth. "It's late, and I'm even more tired now. I think we should go."

"Okay. I'm wiped out myself. Long day. I was rehearsing with my band before I came to the studio to see you."

"Are you making a new album?"

"No. We're rehearsing for tour," he clarifies. "Hit the road next month."

"Oh," I respond quietly as we make our way to Colt's car. I'm already disappointed that he'll be leaving soon, and I only just met him. Now, I have a better idea of how awful it must have been for my mama every time my daddy walked out the door to go play gigs. And the pain must have been unbearable for her when he left and never came back.

"But we can video chat whenever we want to. That's the beauty of the Internet," Colt says when we get in the car.

"Yeah," I agree with the best smile I can muster up. But I'm not so sure. I really like him, but what would it be like to date someone who's never around? Could I trust him? Maybe this is just a friend thing, and he's only being nice because we have the same management. Maybe he doesn't like me as more than a pal.

But then he leans over, and his lips meet mine. The kiss is sweet at first, then grows stronger and more passionate. I don't want him to stop, so I run my fingers through his hair, and we keep on smooching for a little while.

"I really like you, Ollie," Colt confesses when he eventually pulls back.

A goofy grin dances across my lips. "I like you, too."

How quickly everything has changed, but I'm starting to get used to that by now.

Colt drives me home and sends me on my way with one last electric kiss. I remain on my doorstep after his car disappears into the night, that kiss still lingering on my lips. Reluctantly, I unlock the door and slip into the quiet house, tiptoeing past the living room so I won't wake Brett. When I reach my bedroom, I wish Kat were there so I could tell her all about my night. I check my phone, but she hasn't replied. In a daze, I sit down on my bed and take my shoes off. I still can't quite wrap my mind around the night I had. I gently touch my lips, remembering what Colt's kisses felt like. Then, out of nowhere, I wish I had kissed Jack instead. I wish he had asked me out after we recorded our demo. I curl up under the covers and start to cry.

Twenty Seven

Two weeks later, not much has changed. Colt and I spend time together a few times a week, which includes steamy make-out sessions that definitely give me the experience I've been lacking in that department. They're fun, and I'm certainly not complaining about the addition of such a hot guy to my life, but I like hanging out with Jack more. Honestly, I really do adore Colt, and if I didn't know Jack, I'd probably be pursuing Colt like a cat chasing a mouse. But as fond as I am of him, something is missing.

A couple days ago, Erica arrived in town to see Jack before she has to go back to school. She's staying at a hotel nearby, and as long as she's in town, I'm not kicking Colt to the curb. If Jack has someone, then I do, too. It's as simple as that. Plus, Colt and I have that Georgia connection, and we've become good friends.

My mama is still poking around, and her questions about Kat are relentless. Kat still hasn't come back. At least she had the decency to respond to my text messages to let me know she's okay, but I haven't heard her voice or seen her face in weeks. It's unsettling to say the least. I just want to scoop her up in a hug and help her, but as long as she stays away, she's shutting me out. Brett doesn't seem too worried about her absence, which leads me to believe that he knows where she is and that they're in contact. On more than one occasion, I've seen him take off in his car after midnight and not come home until we're all around the table eating breakfast. He usually claims he was out early for a run, but I know better because he comes home in the same clothes as the night before.

I don't have a lot of time to play detective, though. Jack and I are busy with photo shoots and interviews that Will and Alyssa set up to try to get us some exposure while they shop our demo around. We rehearse every day to make sure we're ready to perform if the record labels come calling. And we spend a few hours each day working on new music. Those are the best times because Jack and I are alone to do what we love, making music together.

In my bedroom, I'm listening to Carrie Underwood when someone starts banging on the door. I bolt upright, then go to see what all the ruckus is about.

Jack thunders through as soon as I crack the door open and envelopes me in a huge hug. "We did it!" he shouts. "We did it!"

I have no idea what he means, but I love being in his arms. "What are you talking about?"

He steps back and reveals the biggest grin I've ever seen. "Will just called. We're doing a showcase!"

"No!"

"Yes!"

"I don't believe it!" I yank Jack into another hug. "This is what we've wanted for so long!" The tears are flowing again, but they're happy ones this time.

We both lean back, and Jack wipes a tear from my eye.

"So, what are the details?" I continue, wanting all the information. "When is it? Who's coming? What should I wear?"

He laughs. "You can worry about your outfit later. Will said five labels will be there, some producers, promoters, booking agents, and some people from music publishing companies."

"Wow," I manage. Heat rushes through my body, and I feel lightheaded, so I sit down on the edge of my bed.

"Hey," Jack says, parking himself next to me. "What is it?"

"I'm scared," I admit softly.

He places his hand on my shoulder. "It'll be okay. We'll perform like we would anywhere else, like we did at Atlanta Idol. We can do this."

I inhale and exhale slowly. "You're right. We've got this."

"That's the spirit." Jack gets up, and when he reaches the door, he spins around. "I know you like to figure your clothes out with your mom, so you better get on that. The showcase is in two days. No time to waste." And with that, he shuts the door behind him and he's gone, leaving me alone to thank God for such a wonderful blessing.

"Dear Lord, thank you for giving us this opportunity. Please guide me and Jack through this ordeal. I'm so nervous. But please allow us to sing well, so that we can continue to share our music. Amen."

Now, it's time to find my mama and go shopping. We have work to do.

On the morning of our showcase, I wake up in a fog. It takes me a few seconds to remember where I am and what day it is. The cold medicine I took the night before must have really knocked me out. I had been feeling like I was coming down with something, so I wanted to nip it in the bud. But I realize rather quickly that I haven't fended it off. My body feels like it's been hit by a truck, and when I try to let out a moan of discomfort, I can't. Panic surges through me. My nightmare is coming true. I lost my voice. Despite my aches and pains, I rush out of my room and find my mama, Jack, and Brett in the kitchen. Immediately upon seeing them, I burst into tears.

Mama puts her coffee cup down and hurries to my side. "What's the matter, baby?"

I just shake my head, sobbing in silence.

"Talk to me," she presses on. "Say something."

I lock eyes with her, hoping she'll understand. As the seconds tick by without any words from my mouth, I finally see the recognition and disappointment in her eyes.

"Oh, no," she whispers.

Jack steps forward. "You lost your voice?"

I nod as more tears trickle down my face. "I'm so sorry," I mouth.

My mama grabs some paper towels to wipe my face. "Jack, call Will or Alyssa and ask them for a doctor recommendation. They've lived here longer than y'all. If there's any chance of performing tonight, Ollie needs to get help right away," she instructs him.

He jets off to his room to make the call with Brett right behind him. Alone with my mama, I fall to pieces in her arms.

"I know, baby. But try not to cry. You'll only make it worse." She runs her fingers through my hair. "Hush, baby. It's okay."

The next few hours are a blur of doctors' offices. First, I'm examined by a general physician, then I'm sent to a specialist, then to get X-rays, then back to the specialist. Luckily, the doctors in Music City are used to seeing a lot of cases of laryngitis since so many singers live here. The good news is that it appears that I only have a bad cold, not the flu, and there aren't any signs of bronchitis or pneumonia. The bad news is that I definitely lost my voice because, according to the doctor, I overdid it in rehearsals and pushed my voice too much, spraining one of my vocal chords, which caused inflammation. To get the swelling down, I'm given a cortisone shot and assured that I'll be ready to perform in time for the showcase at seven o'clock.

My mama and Alyssa accompany me to visit the doctors. They both ask a ton of questions to make sure they know exactly what I should and shouldn't do. Aside from only being allowed to rehearse one song with Jack before the show instead of our whole five song set, I'm on complete vocal rest. No talking, no singing, no humming, no whispering. Nothing. I am to shut my mouth and throw away the key, a challenging task for such a chatterbox like me.

At six o'clock, I'm in a tiny theater downtown about to rehearse with Jack. The dress my mama and I picked out is adorable. It has an onyx and taupe zigzag print on a silky fabric. The one-shoulder silhouette has a ruffled detail flowing down the side, and a sparkly, banded waist. My chocolate-colored cowgirl boots and bold bangles on my wrists accessorize the look. Jack is as handsome as ever in a black, button-down shirt, dark jeans, and his signature coffee-brown cowboy boots.

With the hope that she'll show up tonight, I text message Kat several times to come support me. I also want her to style my hair, but when all I receive is a message that says, "Good luck," in return, my mama helps me fix my tresses instead. I'm disappointed, but with everything else going on, my voice is my main concern, not Kat's disappearing act. She really has some explaining to do, though.

Jack and I stand side by side backstage about ready to go on for our one rehearsal number. I keep praying over and over again that my voice will be okay. Well, not just okay. I need it to be amazing, or our chance is blown. Will my voice hold up for five songs in a row? I don't want to imagine the humiliation I'll feel if it gives out in front of the record executives.

"I want to tell you something," Jack announces, taking both my hands into his.

"Okay."

He stares into my eyes. "You're the strongest girl I know. A lot of people would have given up after the kind of setback you had today. But you're pushing through, and that's one of the many things I admire about you." He pauses and gives me a warm smile. "You mean a lot to me, and no matter what happens out there tonight, it's always going to be you and me. If these people don't offer us a record deal, then so be it. We'll try again. We'll keep trying and keep going. Adlenna is here to stay."

My eyes well with tears after hearing such sweet words. Since I'm not supposed to talk, and he knows that, I thank him the best way I know how. When we embrace, I feel safe. I know he means what he said and that he isn't going to hold it against me if something goes wrong with my voice. It's in God's hands now. We did everything we could to prepare for this and overcame all obstacles thrown in our way. It's time to do our best, and let the chips fall where they may.

Twenty Eight

"Ollie?" Jack hollers. "Are you bringing sunscreen?" Seconds later, he appears in the doorway of my bedroom. "You know how my fair skin burns." He flashes a toothy grin my way.

"Poor baby," I tease. "Yes, I have some in my bag."

"Nice. Thanks." He flops down on my beanbag chair. "You about ready to get going? Erica should be here any minute."

I cringe. "She's coming with us?"

"Well, yeah. She's still in town."

"Are y'all officially back together?" I hold my breath for the answer.

He shakes his head. "Nah, we're both in different places in our lives. She's heading off to college, and I'm doing the music thing. Dating wouldn't make a whole lot of sense right now. We're just having a good time until she leaves."

I exhale a sigh of relief. "And when will that be? I thought she was leaving after the showcase."

"So did I, but then Alyssa invited her to the barbeque today, so she extended her trip."

I'll have to remember to thank Alyssa later for that. *Not*. We were all asked to go to Will's and

Alyssa's house for a "Welcome to Nashville" party for me and Jack. It's been five days since the showcase, and the record labels are still silent. My voice made it through that night, and Jack and I are pleased with the show we put on. We got some encouraging feedback, but we haven't heard a thing since then. We're still hopeful, but a bit discouraged, so I suspect that Will and Alyssa are throwing this get-together to get our spirits up.

Oddly enough, my mama and Brett are going to meet up with us at the party because Brett asked her to go shopping with him for new clothes for a job interview. She's certainly warmed up to him, which is a good thing, especially since there's a possibility that he's the father of her grandchild. Oh, Lord.

When Jack and I arrive at Will's and Alyssa's house, we ring the doorbell, but there's no answer.

"They must be out back, so they can't hear us," I say.

Jack nods, agreeing with me.

We head around the side of the house to the gate and let ourselves in. As soon as we round the corner, a big crowd of people yell, "Surprise!"

I'm confused. We know about the barbeque, so what's the surprise? Then, I notice a huge banner hanging across the back wall that reads, "Congratulations to Adlenna, Country Music's Newest Recording Artists!"

My jaw drops. I turn to Jack, and his eyes are bugged out. We both look to Will and Alyssa who stand by with enormous grins on their faces, nodding like crazy.

Alyssa runs over to me and enfolds me in a bear hug. "We got the word this morning. You've been offered a record deal! We wanted to surprise you!"

I'm still resting my voice and trying to be careful not to injure it again, so I don't scream, even though I want to. Instead, I jump in the air and squeal, then immediately turn to Jack who takes me into his arms. Over his shoulder, I see Hanna and Ryder in the crowd, smiling up a storm.

"Hanna!" I exclaim. "You're here!"

Jack and I part, and I rush over to Hanna while he greets Ryder.

"We just got into town. I'm so glad we're here to celebrate your big day! This is incredible, Ollie!" She squeezes me tight, and I'm reminded of how much I've missed her.

My life has completely changed in such a short amount of time. It's surreal. Will and Alyssa pull me and Jack aside to explain that we'll officially sign the contract at their office on Monday with a lawyer present. They made all the necessary arrangements, and they're getting everything in line for us. Jack and I are so lucky to have them on our side. Alyssa also mentions that the label is anxious to release new music from us as soon as possible. Apparently, our popularity is growing by leaps and bounds on the Internet. The views of our Atlanta Idol performances continue to skyrocket, and they want to keep the momentum going. My mama joins the conversation, as well as Jack's parents who flew in just a few hours ago. Everyone we know and love is here to support us, except Kat. And Colt told me he'd be late because he has to rehearse.

Out of the corner of my eye, I spot a man who looks exactly like my daddy. I do a double take and get that déjà vu feeling, but this is unlike the time onstage at Atlanta Idol. This time, it really is him. My mama follows my stare and gasps so loud that Alyssa's usually lethargic cat takes off running.

"Who is that?" Jack wonders.

Unable to find the words, my mama answers for me. "That. Is. Ollie's. Father." She can barely get it out. It's like seeing a ghost.

Heart thundering and legs shaking, I inch my way towards him. "Daddy?" I squeak.

"Hey there, angel face," he says in that gravelly voice that instantly brings back memories I've tried to bury. "I've missed you."

Part of me wants to leap into his arms, but most of me is so darn angry with him. He deserted us, and my heart is still broken.

"How did you know I was here?"

"I told him."

The crowd parts, revealing my runaway sister standing behind my daddy.

"Kat?" I glare at her in utter disbelief.

She always tells me to forget about Daddy whenever I bring him up, and now she's the one to bring him here? Has she lost her marbles?

"How… Why…" She's rendered me speechless…again.

"What's the meaning of all this?" Mama asks, finding her voice. "You don't belong here, Doug. Get out." Her steely-eyed glower is scary. She means business.

"Stop it, Mama," Kat pleads. "I've been staying with Daddy. Give him a chance."

"Kat came to me. I didn't impose," my daddy explains. "She wanted answers. She needed me." He straightens his posture and stands his ground. "I still love our girls with all my heart."

"You sure have a lousy way of showing it," my mama snaps. She locks eyes with Kat. "Why did you seek him out? Why didn't you ask me for help if you needed it? I've *always* been there for you."

"This is different. I wanted to know how he could leave his children. I wanted to know how he felt after he gave us up." She's on the verge of tears.

My mama's eyes widen with a mixture of confusion and pain. "Why are you opening old wounds?"

Tears stream down Kat's face. "I didn't know what to do!" She looks down. "I'm pregnant."

"No. This can't be," my mama protests, immediately in denial. Her face scrunches up from anger. "Wait until I get my hands on that Sutter. I'll wring his neck!"

I know the truth. "Don't say that, Mama. Sutter's not to blame." That last part just slipped out, but I'm actually glad it did.

Everything needs to be out in the open. Besides, we're already putting on quite a show for all the party guests who gape at us in silent shock.

"Miss Jolene," Brett starts, stepping forward. He knows, and the look on his face confirms it. He's about to confess to my mama. Lord, help us all.

"Brett, no," Kat says, grabbing his hand.

"We have to tell her," he whispers to Kat. "Miss Jolene," he starts again, "I'm the father of Kat's child."

There are collective gasps from around the yard. Kat ruined everything. This is supposed to be a happy occasion to celebrate the amazing achievement that Jack and I have reached. But now it's all about her. She humiliated me and my mama. I can't believe she brought my daddy here and confessed that she's pregnant in front of everyone. One look at my mama's devastated expression, and I feel physically sick. My heart aches for her, and I think I might throw up. I can't take it anymore. Thankfully, Colt walks through the gate, so I run to him.

"Sorry I'm late," he apologizes. "What's going on?"

"You're right on time. Get me out of here now," I demand.

"Why?"

"Now, Colt. *Please.*"

He drapes his arm around me and ushers me out of the backyard. The last thing I hear is Erica telling Jack, "It's better that she leaves. Her whole family is a mess."

I'm too embarrassed to turn around and see Jack's reaction, so I just keep on going.

Sitting at the end of the dock, I stare out at the lake. The calm of the water helps me relax. Colt took me here last week, and I loved it, so I asked him to bring me again. The lake house is owned by Colt's family's friends and former neighbors in Macon, an older couple without any children. He said it's their summer home, but they've gone down to Florida for a few weeks.

On the car ride over, I rehashed what happened at Will's and Alyssa's house. Colt listened patiently, but I wonder if my long, drawn-out story annoyed him, even though he didn't let on to feeling that way. Since he's five years older than me and already in his twenties, I often question if I'm too young for him. This incident doesn't help. I don't want him to see me cry. Maybe it's immature to run away like I did. I have no idea what he thinks. Why does his opinion even matter? I don't like him *that* much. The confusion tires me out, so I try to focus on the slight rise and fall of the water to clear my mind.

"Hey," a familiar voice greets me from behind.

I turn my head slightly as Jack sits down next to me with his guitar in hand. "Hey."

"Colt called me and said he drove you here. He was just on his way out when he let me in. He has to go back to rehearsal." Jack pauses for a minute. "I would have taken you home if you hadn't run out so fast."

"I didn't want to go home." I stare straight ahead, avoiding eye contact. "Besides, Erica was with you."

"I told her to go on home." He swings his legs back and forth over the edge of the dock. "Back to Carolina," he clarifies.

"Really?" I finally meet his eyes.

"Mmhmm. It was time."

"So, what happened after I left?"

"Let's see." He lets out a long sigh. "Alyssa and my mom brought your mom in the house. They'll take good care of her. Brett and Kat took off together. And your dad left, too."

"That's what he does best."

"Ollie, I'm sorry. I—"

"No. It's okay." I concentrate on the water again. "Erica was right. My family is a mess."

"You heard her say that?" he asks in surprise.

I nod.

"She had no right to pass judgment like that. No one's family is perfect." He grabs a stray pebble from the dock and throws it into the lake. "I'm sorry I brought her around. She isn't the easiest person to get along with."

I shrug, not wanting to talk about Erica anymore.

"Permission to approach the lake?" Hanna's voice is unmistakable.

"Oh, yeah," Jack remembers with a grin. "Hanna and Ryder came with me."

I twist around and greet her with an inviting smile. "Permission granted."

Hanna and Ryder join us, each taking a seat beside us. I'm really glad to see Hanna. She knows my family as well as I do, so if there's anyone who has any idea what I'm going through, it's her.

"Brett really kicked up a ruckus," Ryder comments, breaking the silence.

"Ain't that the truth," Hanna agrees. "They all did."

I roll my eyes. "I don't want to talk about it or think about it. I want to have some fun. I got a record deal today, y'all!"

Jack chuckles. "I got one, too! Imagine that." He picks up his guitar. "Let's sing something."

"I don't think I should," I say, still worried about my voice.

"Then, I'll sing to you. This little ditty is called, 'Tupelo Honey.'" He begins playing and singing the song made famous by Van Morrison.

We look into each other's eyes, and he sings directly to me, chorusing that I'm an angel as sweet as Tupelo honey. Flooded with memories, I wish we were still on that road trip to Tupelo. All I want is to be with Jack, and come Monday we'll officially be a duo, though no piece of paper could ever compare to the bond we've already formed. From Atlanta Idol until now and into the future, we're in this together for better or worse.

When Jack finishes the song, we all applaud.

"It's hot out here," Ryder complains. "Let's go in the lake."

"We didn't bring swimsuits," Hanna points out.

Ryder eyes her from head to toe. "That don't matter."

She shoves his arm and laughs. "Okay, I won't be a spoil sport. I'm going in but not totally commando." She and Ryder get to their feet to take everything but their undergarments off. "Y'all in or what?" she queries me and Jack.

We reluctantly stand up, stripping articles of clothing from our bodies until all that's left are Jack's black boxer briefs and my hot pink bra and matching panties.

"Ready?" Jack asks me with a playful grin.

I stare into his alluring, azure eyes. "I was born ready."

"On three," Ryder announces.

Jack grabs my hand, I hold onto Hanna's with my other hand, and she takes Ryder's with her free hand. We form a line, surveying the lake beneath us.

"One…two…three!" we count in unison.

And then we jump.

Acknowledgments

Thank you to my mom, Rachel Scrofano, and my dad, Ron Scrofano, for everything.

Tracy Heffner, thank you for reading and editing an early draft of this novel, offering a Southern perspective, and always cheering me on.

Lucie Simone, I'm so glad you're in my corner. I'm amazed by how much support and encouragement you send my way. Thank you so much!

Julie Laird and Gina Marinello-Sweeney, your enthusiasm for my stories never goes unnoticed. I appreciate all that you do. You're awesome!

Thank you to the country music artists who inspired this novel, especially Lauren Alaina and Scotty McCreery.

Shout out to the cast of *Austin & Ally* (Ross Lynch, Laura Marano, Raini Rodriguez, and Calum Worthy) for showing people that good, clean fun is still cool. And to everyone involved in the making of *Austin & Ally*, thank you for portraying teenagers in a positive light. Your work is inspiring.

A huge thanks to the incredibly supportive community of authors who always have words of encouragement throughout the grueling publishing process.

To my readers, thank you! Your support means so much to me, and I am forever grateful.

About the Author

NANCY SCROFANO is the author of *True Love Way* and *Cupid On Deck*, as well as short stories in the *Sunlounger* and *Merry & Bright* anthologies. She lives in southern California where she is at work on her next novel. For more information about Nancy, please visit www.nancyscrofano.com.